ULTIMATE PAPER PLANES

MAKE AND LAUNCH INCREDIBLE PLANES!

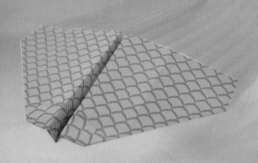

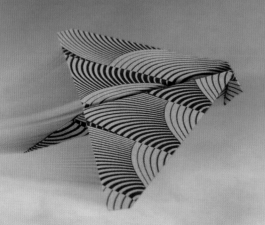

ARCTURUS

This edition published in 2015 by Arcturus Publishing Limited
26/27 Bickels Yard, 151–153 Bermondsey Street,
London SE1 3HA

ISBN: 978-1-78404-285-1
CH004291NT
Supplier 13, Date 0115, Print Run 3817

Models and photography: Michael Wiles
Text: Catherine Ard
Design: Picnic
Edited: Kate Overy

Printed in China

Contents

 **GLIDERS**

STUNTS

 **JETS**

 **SPACE**

Basic folds

This book shows you how to make a fantastic fleet of paper planes. All you need for each amazing model is a sheet of paper, your fingers, and some clever creasing. So, get folding and get flying!

GETTING STARTED

The paper we've used for these planes is thin, but strong, so that it can be folded many times. There are four different-patterned papers included in the book for you to pick from. You can also use ordinary scrap paper cut to 173 x 220 mm (6.8 x 8.6 in), but make sure it's not too thick.

A lot of the planes in this book are made with the same folds. The ones that appear most are explained on these pages. It's a good idea to try out these folds before you start.

KEY

When making the planes, follow this key to find out what the lines, arrows and symbols mean.

.... mountain fold   direction to move paper

– – – – – – – – – valley fold   ◀ ▶ direction to push or pull paper

MOUNTAIN FOLD

To make a mountain fold, fold the paper so that the crease is pointing up at you, like a mountain.

VALLEY FOLD

To make a valley fold, fold the paper the other way, so that the crease is pointing away from you, like a valley.

OUTSIDE REVERSE FOLD

An outside reverse fold can be used to create a plane's nose, as for the Whirlybird on p62.

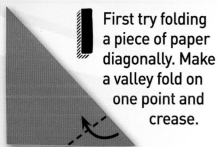

1 First try folding a piece of paper diagonally. Make a valley fold on one point and crease.

2 It's important to make sure that the paper is creased well. Run your finger over the crease two or three times.

3 Unfold and open up the corner slightly. Refold the crease farthest away from you into a valley fold.

OPEN

4 Open up the paper a little more and start to turn the corner inside out. Then close the paper when the fold begins to turn.

5 You now have an outside reverse fold. You can either flatten the paper or leave it rounded out.

FOLDING TIPS

Paper planes are easy to make, and fun to fly, but you need to fold with care if your planes are going to glide, loop, twirl, and dive the way they are meant to.

1 Before you crease the paper, make sure the edges, or points, meet exactly where they are supposed to. Even small overlaps will make the plane hard to fly.

2 Use a ruler to help you line up your creases, especially when you are folding a sharp nose point, or creasing several layers of paper at once.

USE A RULER!

3 The left side of the plane is always a mirror image of the right side of the plane. Carefully line up the second wing to match the first wing.

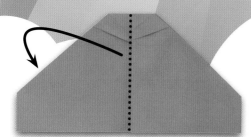

4 Before you fly a plane, check that the wings and wing tips are sitting at the same angle on each side. Crooked wings won't fly!

5

Gliders

Find a big space to send these gliders swooping and swerving.
Catch the wind right and watch them drift off into the distance!

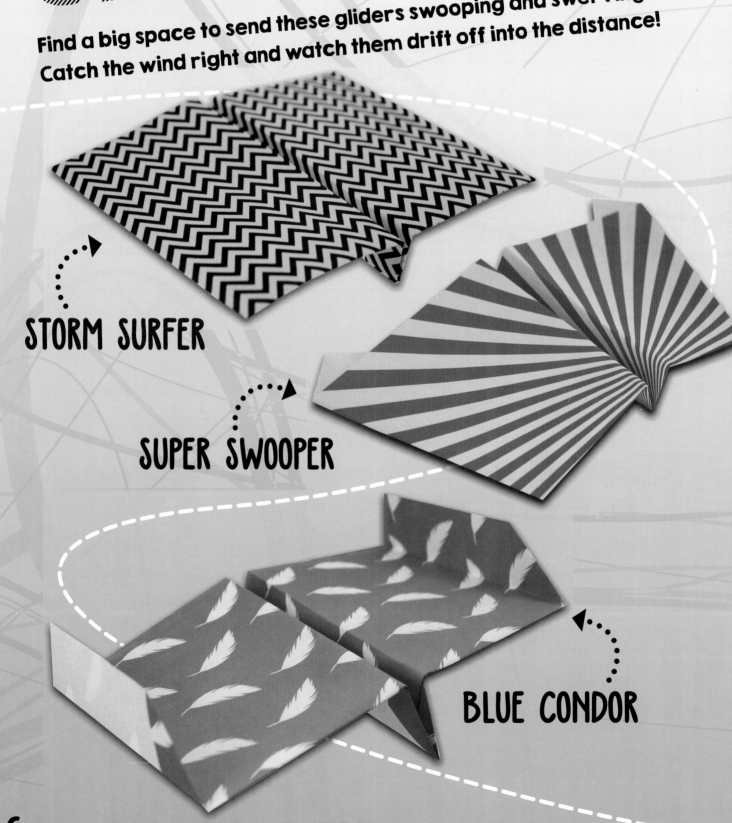

STORM SURFER

SUPER SWOOPER

BLUE CONDOR

6

PTEROSAUR

FOLDING TIP
CHANGE THE ANGLE OF YOUR PLANE'S WINGS TO GET A DIFFERENT RESULT. POINT THE WINGS SLIGHTLY DOWN, SLIGHTLY UP, OR KEEP THEM LEVEL. MAKE SURE BOTH WINGS ARE TILTED THE SAME AMOUNT!

JUNGLE HAWK

SKY RAY

FLYING TIP
GLIDERS' WIDE WINGS AND FLAT SHAPE MEAN THEY NEED A GENTLE THROW. HOLD YOUR PLANE IN FRONT OF YOU, ANGLE IT SLIGHTLY UPWARD AND TOSS IT INTO THE AIR TO SEND IT ON ITS WAY.

WIND RIDER

Storm Surfer

Fold this dazzling zigzag glider to streak through the sky like a bolt from the blue. It's so simple, it will be ready in a flash!

FLASH AND DASH!

FLIP OVER

6 MORE TO GO!

1 Place the paper as shown. Fold over the top a finger's width from the edge.

2 Continue to fold over six more times, keeping the folds even.

3 Turn the paper over.

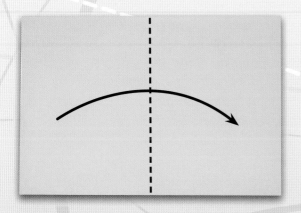

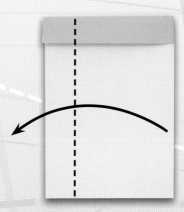

4 Fold the paper in half from left to right.

5 Fold back the top layer to make the first wing.

FOLD BEHIND

OPEN UP

6 Mountain fold the right side, lining it up with the wing you just made.

7 Pinch the paper underneath and pull up the wings.

8 Hold the paper just behind the folded edge. Aim slightly upward and gently throw to let your plane surf and then gently land!

FINISHED!

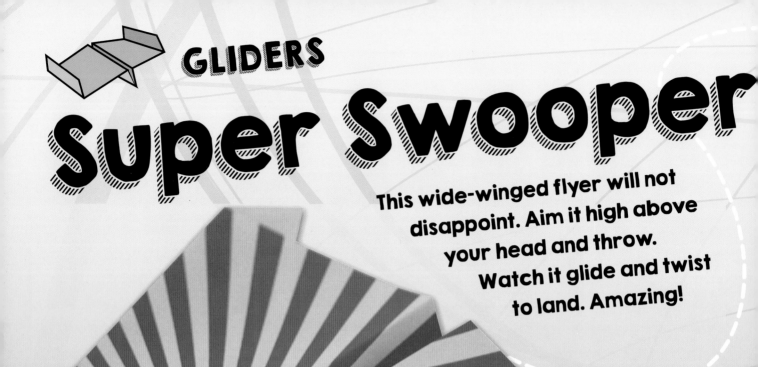

Super Swooper

This wide-winged flyer will not disappoint. Aim it high above your head and throw. Watch it glide and twist to land. Amazing!

DUCK AND DIVE!

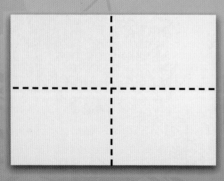

1 Place the paper as shown. Fold it in half from left to right and unfold, then from top to bottom and unfold.

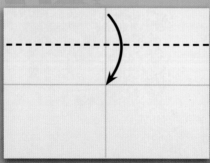

2 Valley fold the top edge to meet exactly on the central crease.

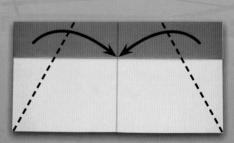

3 Fold in the corners so that the top edges meet on the central crease.

4 Fold the top down.

5 Fold the top down again.

FLIP OVER

6 Turn the paper over.

7 Valley fold the paper in half from left to right.

FOLD BEHIND

8 Fold back the top layer, as shown.

9 Mountain fold the right side behind.

FINISHED!

OPEN UP

10 Pinch the paper underneath and pull up the wings.

11 Your glider should look like this. Hold your plane just behind the nose. Aim it high and let go. Whoosh!

Blue Condor

Wow your friends with this winged wonder. Watch it silently soar, then glide on the wind before sweeping back to earth.

RIDE AND GLIDE!

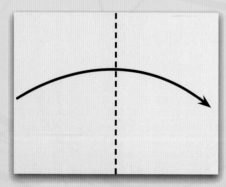

1 Place the paper as shown. Fold it in half from left to right and unfold.

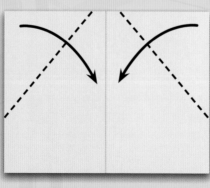

2 Fold the top corners so that the points meet halfway down the central crease.

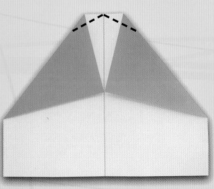

3 Make two angled folds on the top edge, as shown.

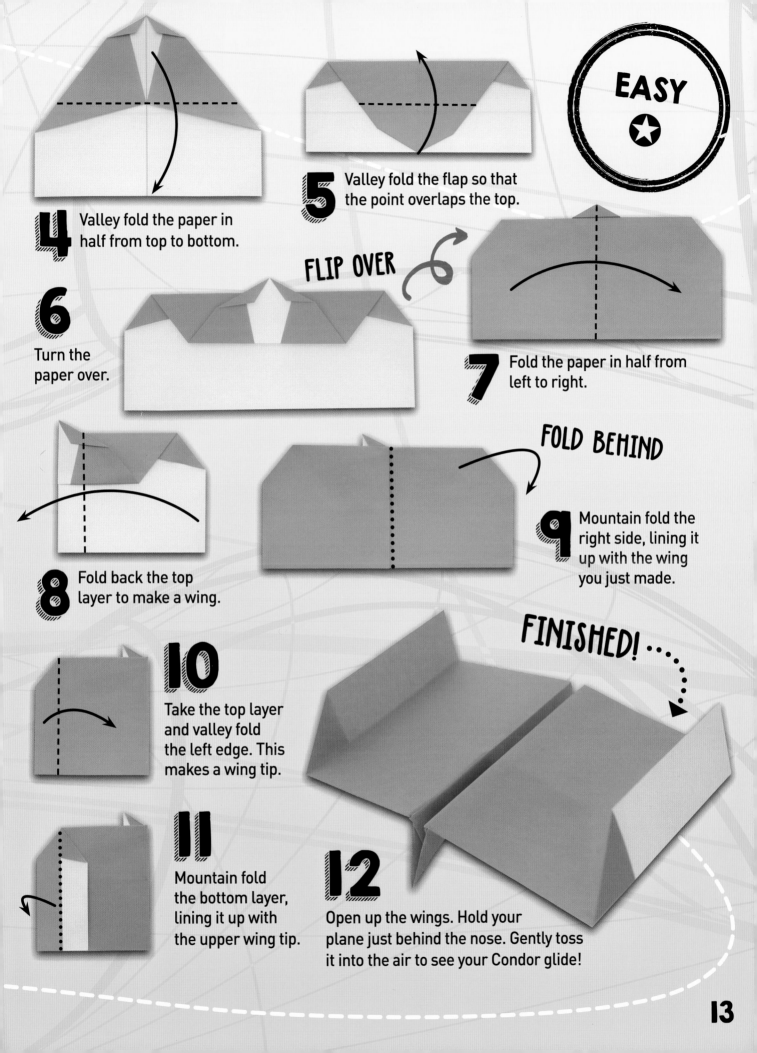

4 Valley fold the paper in half from top to bottom.

5 Valley fold the flap so that the point overlaps the top.

EASY ★

FLIP OVER

6 Turn the paper over.

7 Fold the paper in half from left to right.

8 Fold back the top layer to make a wing.

FOLD BEHIND

9 Mountain fold the right side, lining it up with the wing you just made.

FINISHED!

10 Take the top layer and valley fold the left edge. This makes a wing tip.

11 Mountain fold the bottom layer, lining it up with the upper wing tip.

12 Open up the wings. Hold your plane just behind the nose. Gently toss it into the air to see your Condor glide!

GLIDERS

Pterosaur

Take some gliding tips from fearsome early fliers. With its pointy prehistoric shape this super soarer could be straight out of the Jurassic jungle!

SWOOP AND SOAR!

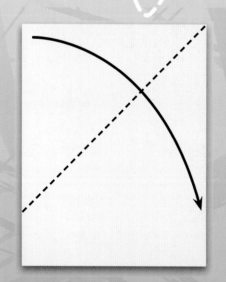

OPEN UP

1 Place the paper as shown. Valley fold the top edge to meet the right-hand edge.

2 Open up the paper.

3 Now valley fold the top edge to meet the left-hand edge.

14

FLIP OVER

4 Open up the paper.

5 You should have a creased cross. Turn the paper over.

6 Valley fold the paper over the middle of the cross.

7 Open up the paper.

8 Turn the paper over.

FLIP OVER

PUSH IN HERE ▼

9 Push in on the central point to make the sides pop up.

GLIDERS

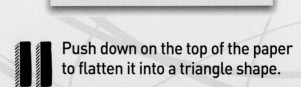

PUSH DOWN HERE

PUSH IN HERE

PUSH IN HERE

10 Push in the sides on the central crease until they collapse.

11 Push down on the top of the paper to flatten it into a triangle shape.

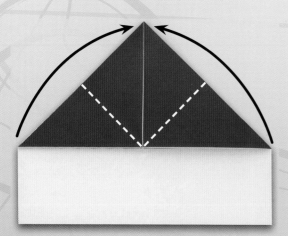

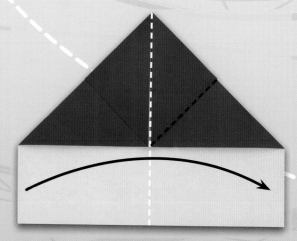

12 Taking the top layers, bring the bottom points up to meet the top point.

13 Valley fold the paper in half from left to right.

14 Fold back the top layer, as shown, to make the first wing.

NOSE

15 Mountain fold the right side, lining it up with the wing you just made. Don't fold the triangular nose.

16 Take the top layer and valley fold the left edge. This makes a wing tip.

FOLD BEHIND

17 Mountain fold the bottom layer, lining it up exactly with the upper wing tip.

18 Pinch the paper underneath and open up the wings. Make sure they are level.

OPEN UP

...FINISHED!

19 Straighten the wing tips. Hold the plane underneath and throw it gently forward to send your Pterosaur soaring!

Jungle Hawk

Go undercover with this stealthy glider!
Take it to a park or field and you can
send it sailing, unseen, among the trees!

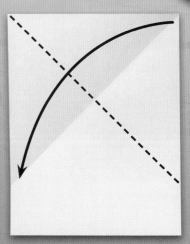

SWIFT AND SILENT!

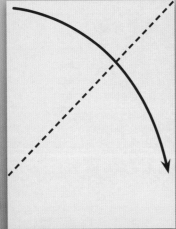

1 Place the paper as shown. Valley fold the top edge to meet the right-hand edge.

2 Open up the paper.

3 Now valley fold the top edge to meet the left-hand edge.

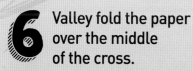
OPEN UP

4 Open up the paper.

You should have a creased cross. Turn the paper over.

FLIP OVER

5 You should have a creased cross. Turn the paper over.

6 Valley fold the paper over the middle of the cross.

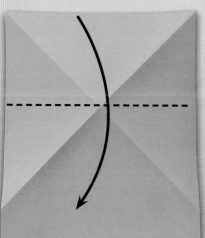

7 Open up the paper once more.

8 Turn the paper over.

FLIP OVER

PUSH IN HERE ▼

9 Push in on the central point to make the sides pop up.

GLIDERS

 PUSH IN HERE ▶

◀ **PUSH IN HERE**

PUSH DOWN HERE ▼

11 Push down on the top of the paper to flatten it into a triangle shape.

10 Push in the sides on the central crease until they collapse.

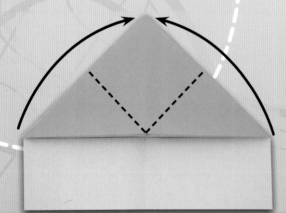

12 Taking the top layers, bring the bottom points up to meet the top point. This makes a square.

13 Fold the bottom left edge of the square to meet the central crease.

14 Open out the fold you just made.

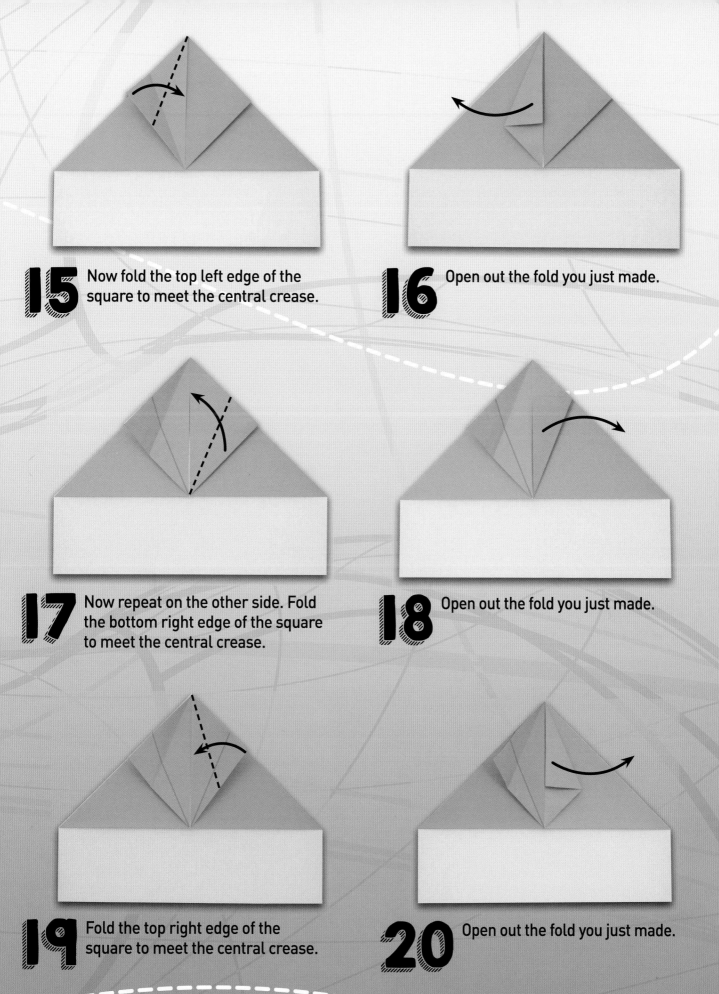

15 Now fold the top left edge of the square to meet the central crease.

16 Open out the fold you just made.

17 Now repeat on the other side. Fold the bottom right edge of the square to meet the central crease.

18 Open out the fold you just made.

19 Fold the top right edge of the square to meet the central crease.

20 Open out the fold you just made.

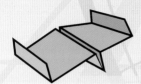

GLIDERS

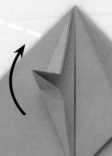

PINCH AND FOLD!

21 Your paper should look like this.

22 On the left side, pinch the corner and fold in along the creases.

23 Flatten the paper to make a triangular flap.

PINCH AND FOLD!

24 Repeat on the other side. Pinch the corner and fold in to make a triangular flap.

FOLD BEHIND

25 Mountain fold the point. Leave the flaps you just made sticking out at the top.

26 Fold the paper in half from left to right.

27

Valley fold the top layer, as shown. This makes the first wing.

28

Mountain fold the other side, lining it up with the wing you just made.

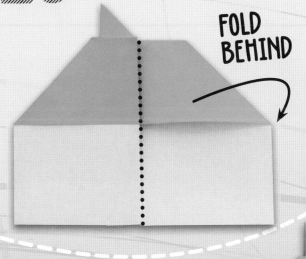

FOLD BEHIND

29

Take the top layer and fold in the left-hand edge to make a wing tip.

30

Mountain fold the bottom layer, lining it up with the upper wing tip.

31

Pinch the paper underneath and open up the wings. Check they are level.

OPEN UP

32

Straighten the wing tips and you are ready for take off. Aim high and toss it into the air!

FINISHED!

GLIDERS
Sky Ray

Fold this great-winged glider right and it will sweep gracefully through the blue, just like a manta ray cruising through the ocean!

SWEEP AND SWERVE!

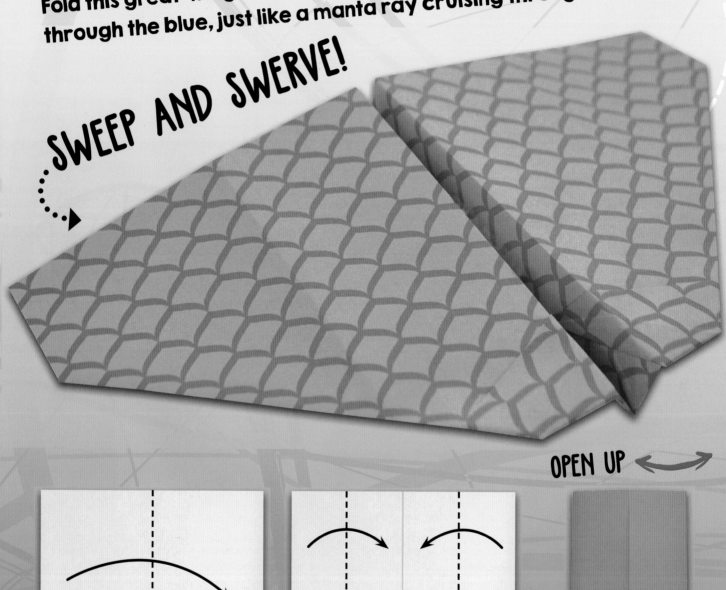

OPEN UP ⟷

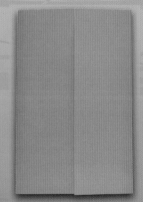

1 Place the paper as shown. Fold it in half from left to right and unfold.

2 Valley fold the sides to meet the central crease.

3 Open up the paper.

24

OPEN UP

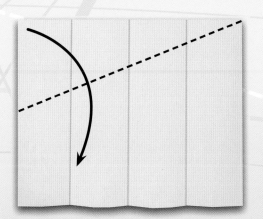

MEDIUM

4 Valley fold the top left corner to meet the first crease in from the left.

5 Open up the paper.

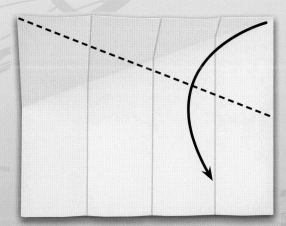

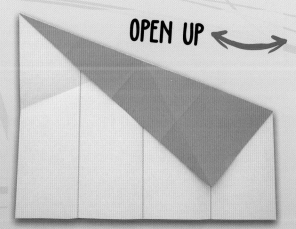
OPEN UP

6 Repeat on the other side. Fold the top right corner to meet the first crease in from the right.

7 Open up the paper.

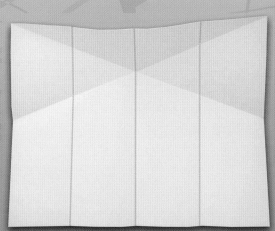

FLIP OVER

8 You should now have a creased cross. Turn the paper over.

9 Valley fold the top edge over the middle of the cross.

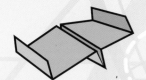

GLIDERS

PUSH IN HERE

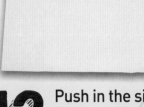

10 Open up the paper once more.

11 Turn the paper over.

12 Push in the sides on the central crease until they collapse.

PUSH DOWN HERE

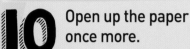

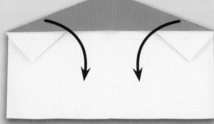

13 Push down on the top of the paper to flatten it into a wide triangle.

14 Fold down the flaps on either side.

15 Turn the paper over.

FLIP OVER

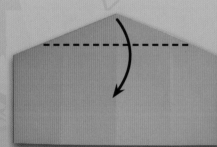

16 Valley fold the top point, as shown.

17 Turn the paper over.

FLIP OVER

18 Fold in the sides along the creases you made earlier.

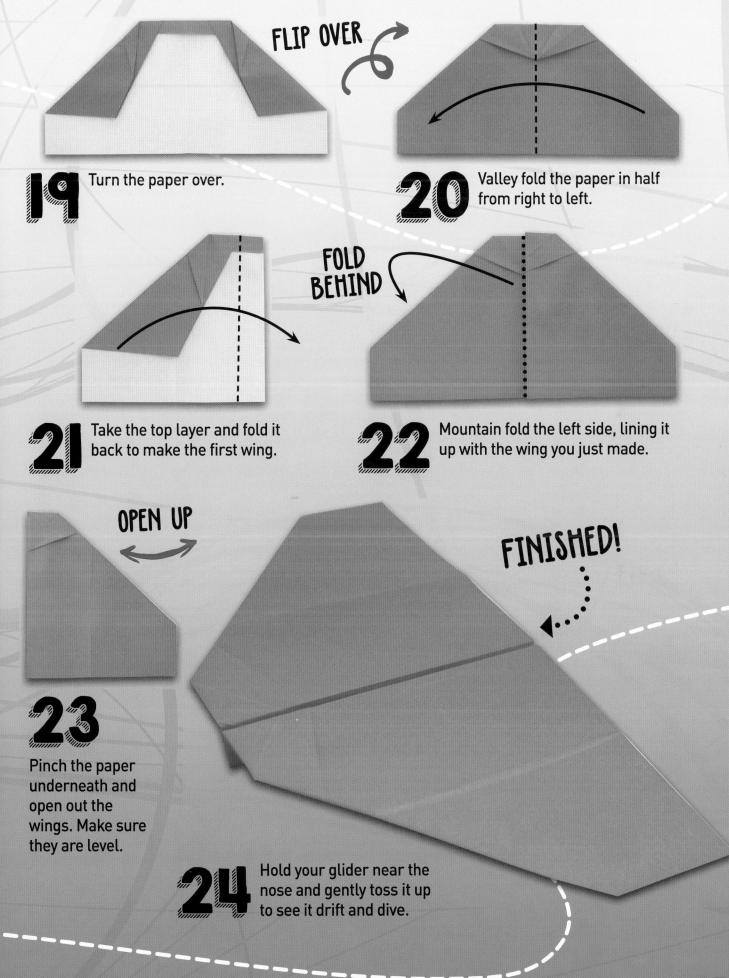

FLIP OVER

19 Turn the paper over.

20 Valley fold the paper in half from right to left.

FOLD BEHIND

21 Take the top layer and fold it back to make the first wing.

22 Mountain fold the left side, lining it up with the wing you just made.

OPEN UP

FINISHED!

23 Pinch the paper underneath and open out the wings. Make sure they are level.

24 Hold your glider near the nose and gently toss it up to see it drift and dive.

GLIDERS
Wind Rider

Prepare to be blown away by this easy-to-fold flyer! Catch the wind right, and watch it breeze effortlessly through the air.

SKIP AND SKIM!

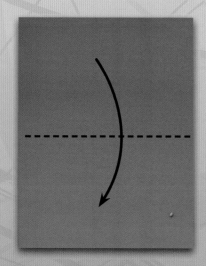

1 Place the paper with the patterned side facing up. Fold it in half from top to bottom.

2 Take the top layer and fold up the edge to fall 15 mm (½ in) from the top.

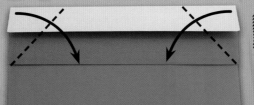

3 Fold over the top edge, as shown.

4 Valley fold the top corners to meet the edge of the flap.

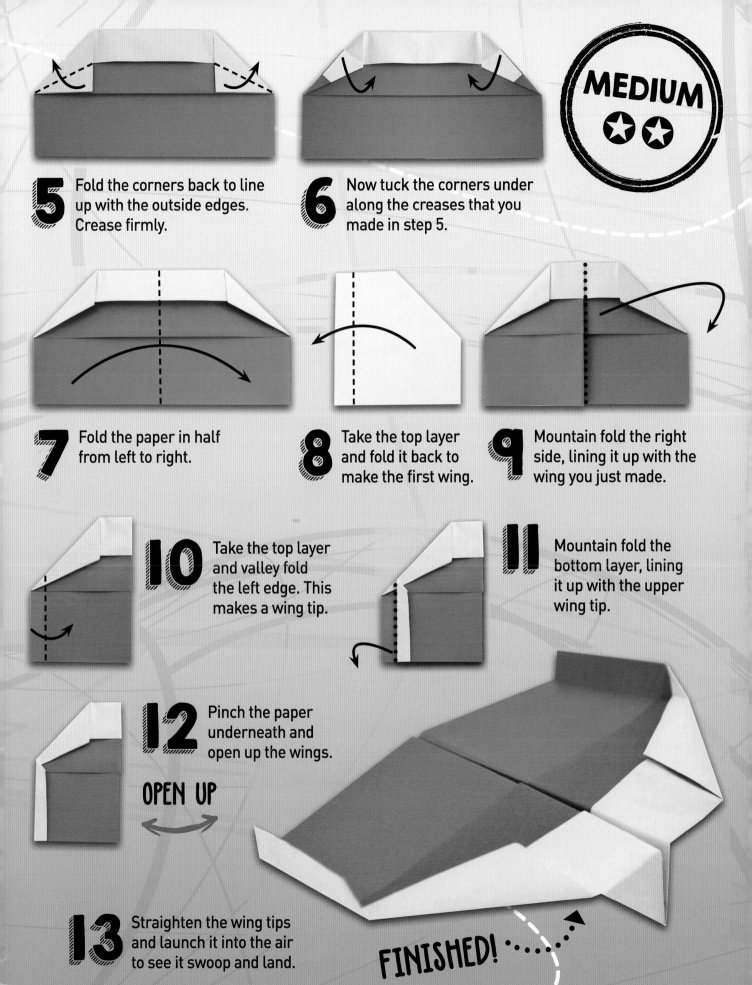

5 Fold the corners back to line up with the outside edges. Crease firmly.

6 Now tuck the corners under along the creases that you made in step 5.

7 Fold the paper in half from left to right.

8 Take the top layer and fold it back to make the first wing.

9 Mountain fold the right side, lining it up with the wing you just made.

10 Take the top layer and valley fold the left edge. This makes a wing tip.

11 Mountain fold the bottom layer, lining it up with the upper wing tip.

12 Pinch the paper underneath and open up the wings.

OPEN UP

13 Straighten the wing tips and launch it into the air to see it swoop and land.

FINISHED!

Jet Planes

These dynamic darts are the rockets of the paper plane world.
They fly fast, not far, so power your launch and let them rip!

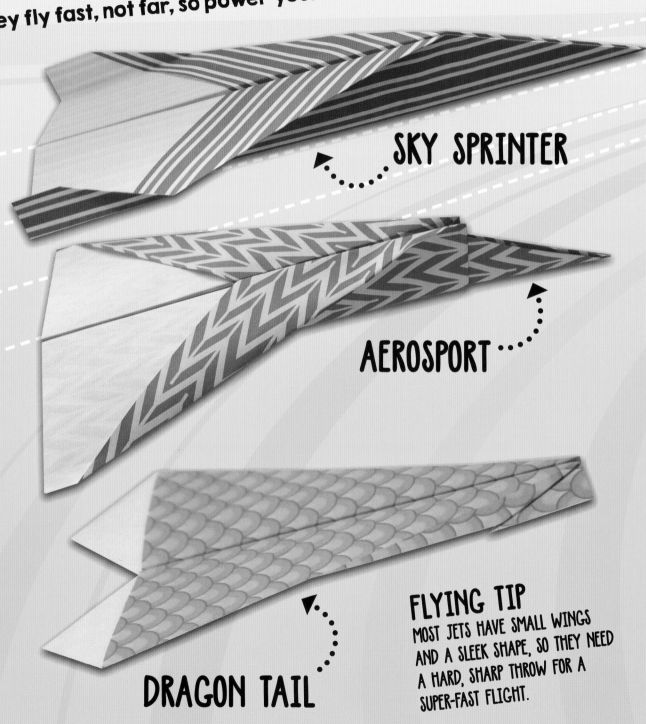

SKY SPRINTER

AEROSPORT

DRAGON TAIL

FLYING TIP
MOST JETS HAVE SMALL WINGS
AND A SLEEK SHAPE, SO THEY NEED
A HARD, SHARP THROW FOR A
SUPER-FAST FLIGHT.

SUPER SPARK

THE PHANTOM

MEGA DART

FLYING TIP
AIM STRAIGHT AHEAD TO GET YOUR
JET TO FLY ON TARGET. THROW
UPWARD AT A 45° ANGLE IF YOU
WANT YOUR JET TO GO FARTHER.

THE STING

Sky Sprinter

This striped speedster certainly knocks spots off other paper planes as it tears through the air. Look sharp and you can fold it in a matter of minutes, then let it fly!

NIP AND ZIP!

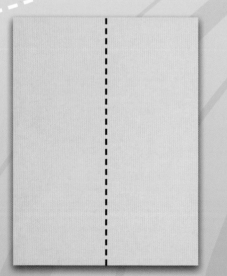

1 Place the paper as shown. Fold it in half from left to right and unfold.

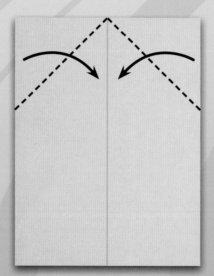

2 Valley fold the top edges to meet on the central crease.

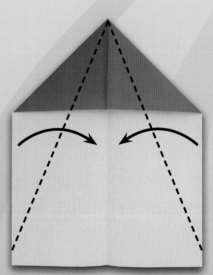

3 Now valley fold the sides so that the patterned edges meet on the central crease.

4 Fold the paper in half from left to right.

5 Take the top layer and fold it back to make the first wing.

6 Mountain fold the right side behind, lining it up with the first wing.

7 Take the top layer and valley fold the left edge to make a wing tip.

8 Mountain fold the bottom layer, lining it up with wing tip you just made.

9 Open up the wings, making sure they are level.

OPEN UP

FINISHED!

10 Straighten the wing tips and hold the plane behind the nose. Now let it go with a strong, straight throw!

 **JETS**

Aerosport

Make this champion flyer and challenge your friends to a jet race. Double-check your folds and you are sure to be first past the flag!

FLING IT AND WIN IT!

1 Place the paper as shown. Fold it in half from left to right and unfold.

2 Valley fold the top edges to meet on the central crease.

3 Valley fold the sides so that the patterned edges meet on the central crease.

4 Fold down the point, as shown.

5 Fold the point back again just below the top edge.

6 Valley fold the paper in half from left to right.

7 Take the top layer and fold it back to make the first wing.

8 Mountain fold the right side behind, lining it up with the first wing.

9 Open up the wings and check they are level.

OPEN UP

FINISHED! ·····

10 Hold your plane just in front of the middle. Pull back and throw strongly and smoothly for a super-fast flight.

 **JETS**

Dragon Tail

This sleek-bodied jet with its legendary forked tail is pure magic to fly. When it comes to speed, it's off the scale!

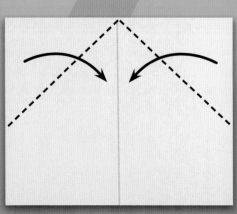

FAST AND FIERY!

 1

Place the paper as shown. Fold it in half from left to right and unfold.

2

Valley fold the top edges to meet on the central crease.

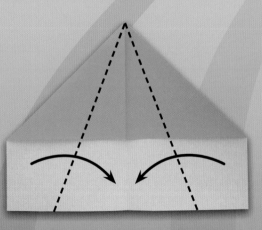

3

Now valley fold the sides to meet on the central crease.

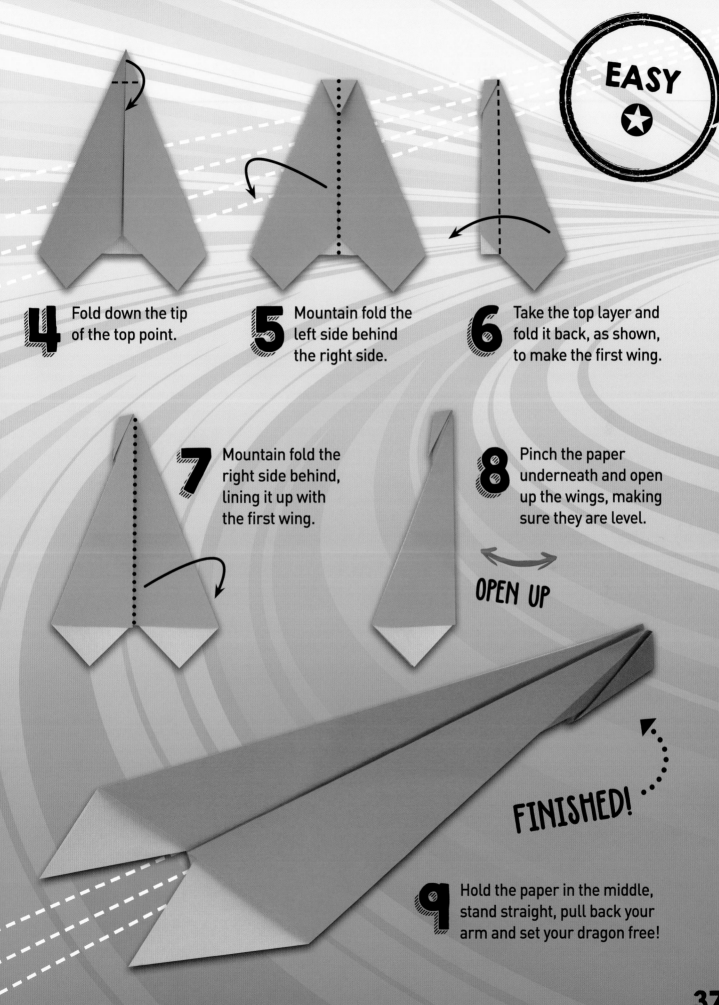

4 Fold down the tip of the top point.

5 Mountain fold the left side behind the right side.

6 Take the top layer and fold it back, as shown, to make the first wing.

7 Mountain fold the right side behind, lining it up with the first wing.

8 Pinch the paper underneath and open up the wings, making sure they are level.

OPEN UP

FINISHED!

9 Hold the paper in the middle, stand straight, pull back your arm and set your dragon free!

 **JETS**

Super Spark

With faultless folds and super-sharp creases, this scorching-hot jet will burn across the sky like a blazing comet. When it comes to cool looks and flashy flights, this jet is on fire!

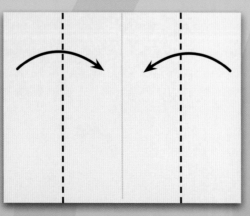

FLASH AND FLARE!

1

Place the paper as shown. If you have a flame design put it at the bottom. Fold the paper in half from left to right and unfold.

2

Valley fold the sides to meet on the central crease.

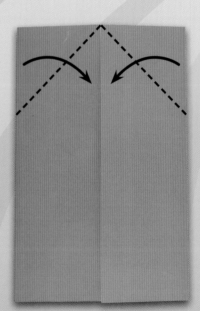

3

Valley fold the top edges to meet on the central crease.

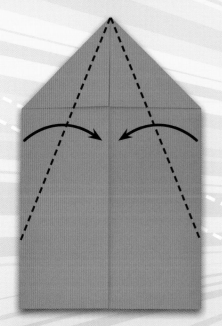

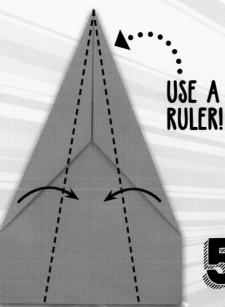

USE A RULER!

5 Fold in the sides once more to meet on the central crease.

4 Fold in the sides to meet on the central crease.

6 Mountain fold the right side behind the left side to make the wings.

7 Pinch the paper underneath and open up the wings on either side.

OPEN UP

FINISHED!

8 Make sure the wings are level and the nose is straight, then aim for the sky and let the Super Spark burn!

The Phantom

Is it a bird? Is it a plane? Keep them guessing with this ultra-fast flyer! Throw it straight and smooth and it will leave the competition trailing in its shadow.

SPOOKILY FAST!

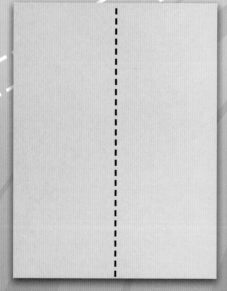

1 Place the paper as shown. Fold it in half from left to right and unfold.

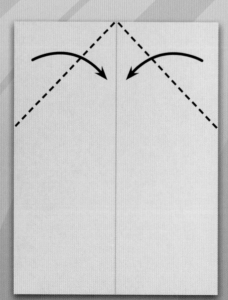

2 Valley fold the top edges to meet neatly on the central crease.

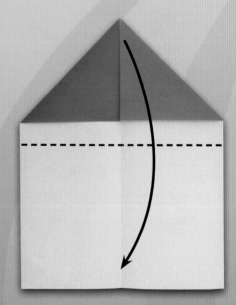

3 Fold down the top point to meet the paper a finger's width from the bottom edge.

40

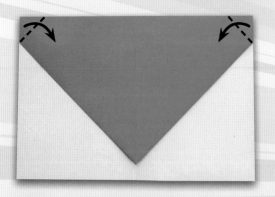
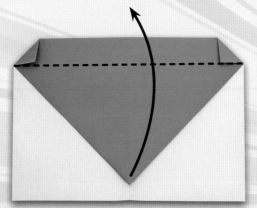

4 Valley fold the tips of the top corners.

5 Fold back the flap, in line with the folded corners.

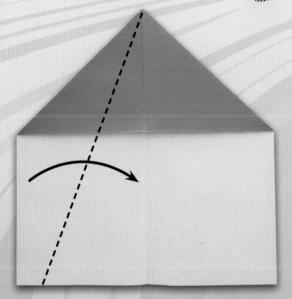
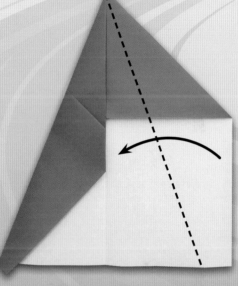

6 Valley fold the left side to meet the central crease.

7 Repeat on the other side to make an arrow shape.

8 Valley fold the paper in half from left to right.

SPOT THE HIDDEN FOLD!

41

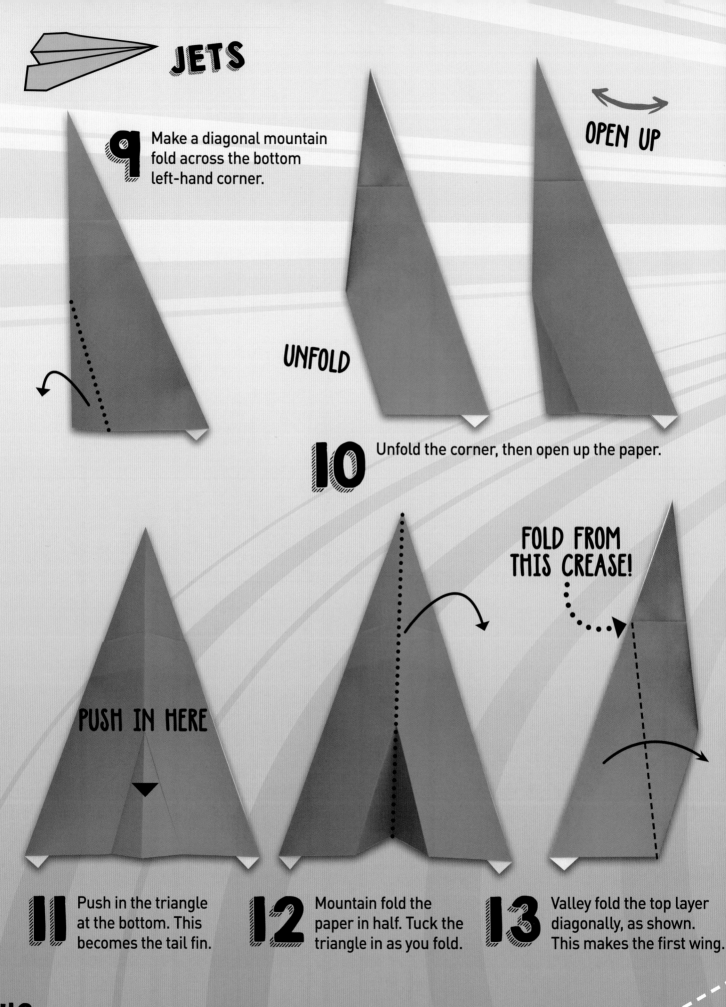

JETS

9 Make a diagonal mountain fold across the bottom left-hand corner.

UNFOLD

OPEN UP

10 Unfold the corner, then open up the paper.

PUSH IN HERE

FOLD FROM THIS CREASE!

11 Push in the triangle at the bottom. This becomes the tail fin.

12 Mountain fold the paper in half. Tuck the triangle in as you fold.

13 Valley fold the top layer diagonally, as shown. This makes the first wing.

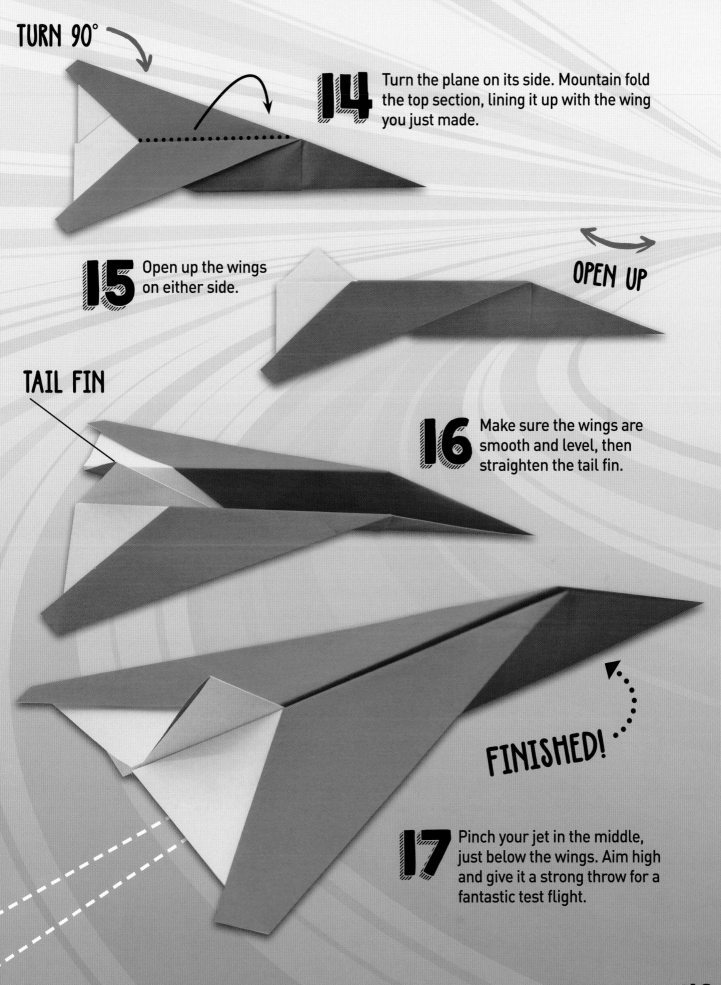

TURN 90°

14 Turn the plane on its side. Mountain fold the top section, lining it up with the wing you just made.

15 Open up the wings on either side.

OPEN UP

TAIL FIN

16 Make sure the wings are smooth and level, then straighten the tail fin.

FINISHED!

17 Pinch your jet in the middle, just below the wings. Aim high and give it a strong throw for a fantastic test flight.

Mega Dart

To be a real jet-flying ace you need to master the Mega Dart.
It's tricky to handle, but perfect your aim and you'll soon be a pro!

SHOOT AND SCORE!

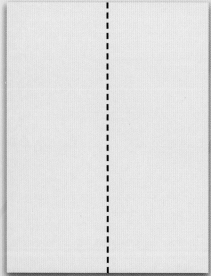

1 Place the paper as shown. Fold it in half from left to right and unfold.

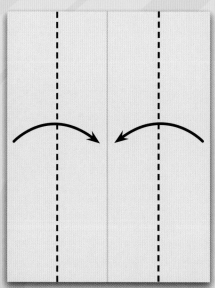

2 Fold in the sides to meet on the central crease.

3 Valley fold the top edges to meet on the central crease.

4

Now valley fold the top edges so they meet in the middle.

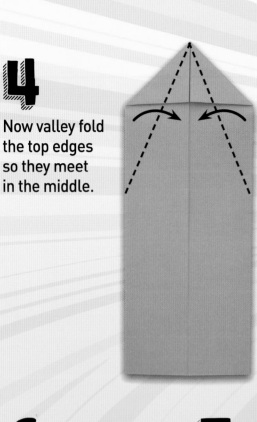

5

Turn the paper over.

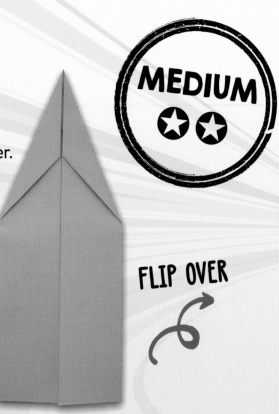

FLIP OVER

6

Fold the paper in half from left to right.

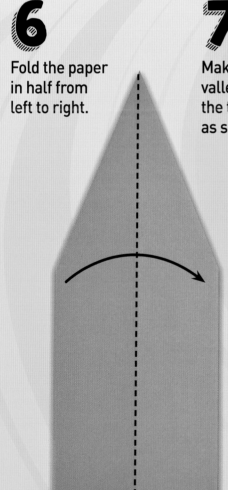

7

Make a diagonal valley fold on the top layer, as shown.

8

Turn the paper over.

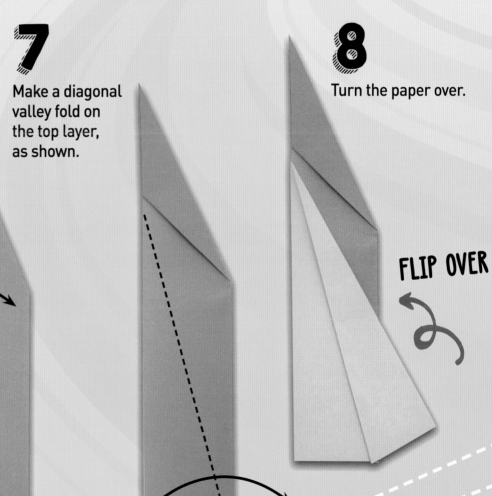

FLIP OVER

 **JETS**

9

Take the top layer and make a diagonal fold. Line the edges up exactly with the other side.

LINE IT UP!

10

Valley fold the bottom corner, as shown.

11

Now mountain fold the corner behind along the same crease. Unfold.

12

Open up the paper.

 OPEN UP

13

Pinch the central crease to pull up the middle section. This is the tail fin. Close the paper with the fin tucked inside.

FIN

FIN

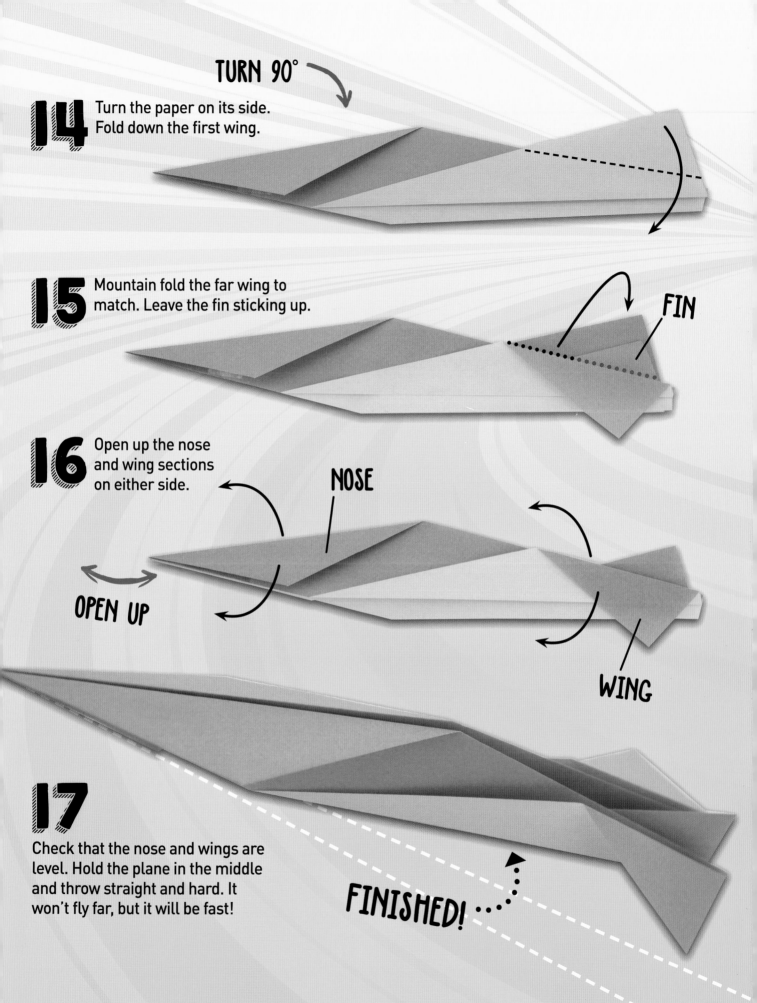

TURN 90°

14 Turn the paper on its side. Fold down the first wing.

15 Mountain fold the far wing to match. Leave the fin sticking up.

FIN

16 Open up the nose and wing sections on either side.

NOSE

OPEN UP

WING

17

Check that the nose and wings are level. Hold the plane in the middle and throw straight and hard. It won't fly far, but it will be fast!

FINISHED!

The Sting

Fly this striking jet and cause a real buzz. With its sharp shape and awesome gliding power, you'll need to make room for its zoom!

POINT AND GO!

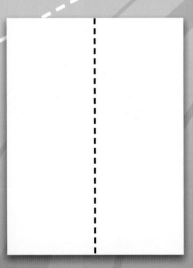

1 Place the paper as shown. Fold it in half from left to right and unfold.

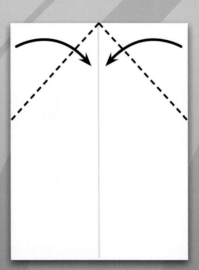

2 Valley fold the top edges to meet on the central crease. This makes a triangle.

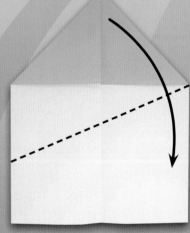

3 Valley fold the right edge of the triangle to meet the right edge of the paper.

4 Open up the paper.

OPEN UP

5 Now fold the left edge of the triangle to meet the left edge of the paper.

6 Open up the paper.

OPEN UP

7 FLIP OVER

You should have a creased cross like this. Turn the paper over.

8 Valley fold the paper over the middle of the cross.

9 Open up the paper.

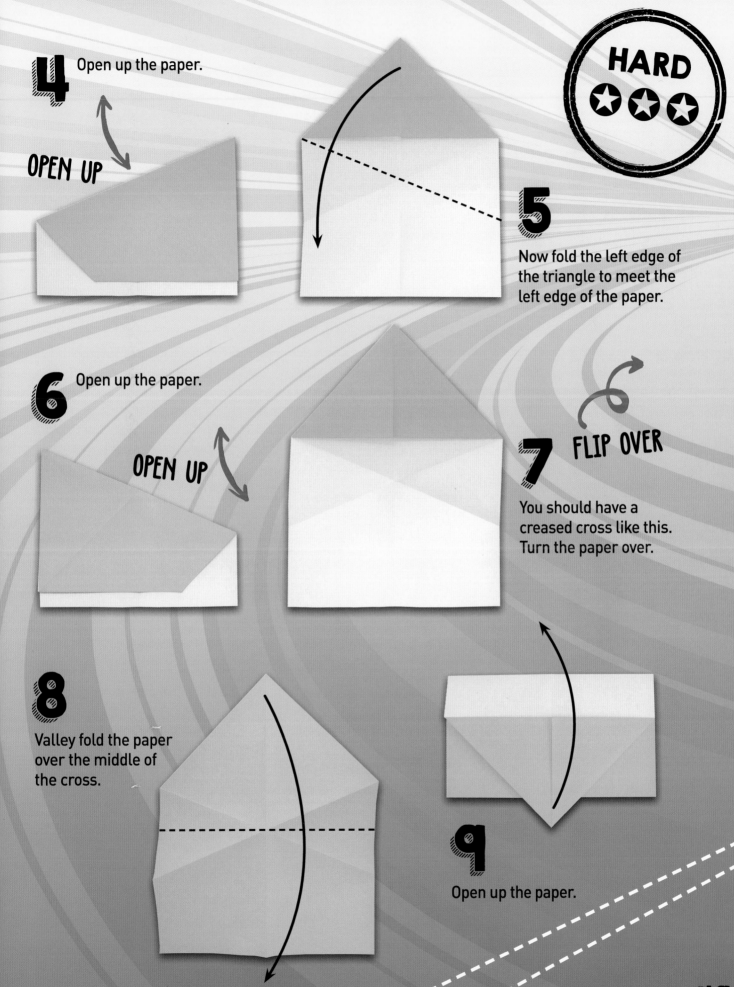

JETS

10

Turn the paper over.

FLIP OVER

PUSH IN

11

Push in the sides on the central crease until they collapse.

12

Fold down the point.

PUSH DOWN HERE

13

Push down on the top of the paper to flatten it into a diamond shape.

14

Valley fold the flap, as shown.

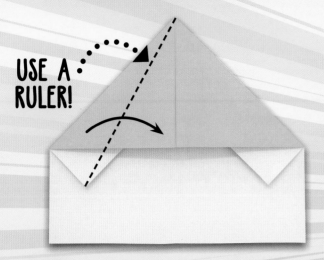

15 Valley fold the left side of the flap from point to point.

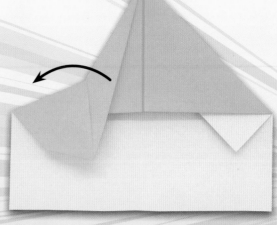

16 Open up the fold you just made.

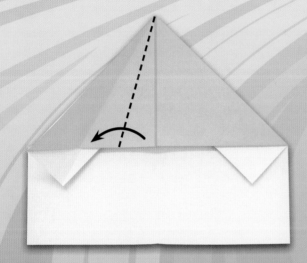

17 Valley fold the inside edge of the flap to meet the crease you just made.

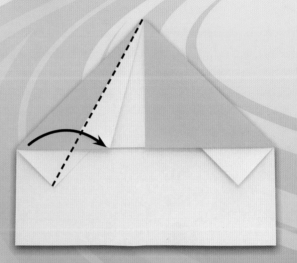

18 Fold over the outside edge along the same crease.

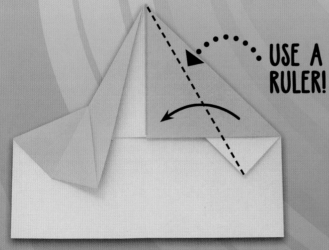

USE A RULER!

19 Now valley fold the right flap from point to point.

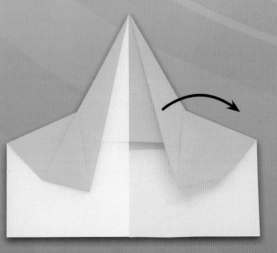

20 Open up the fold you just made.

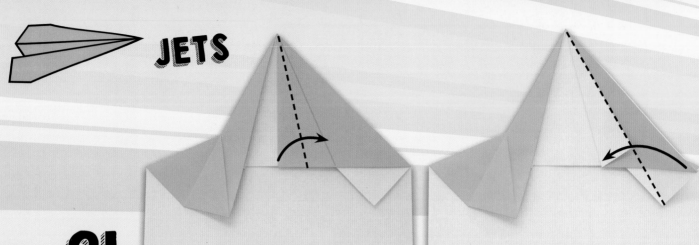

JETS

21

Valley fold the inside edge of the flap to meet the crease you just made.

22

Fold over the outside edge along the same crease.

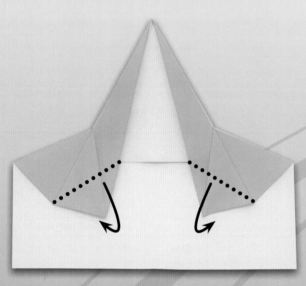

23

Mountain fold the points on either side, tucking them underneath.

24

Mountain fold the right side behind the left side.

25

Make a diagonal crease across the bottom corner. Fold both ways.

26

Open out the fold you just made.

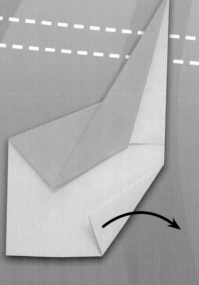

27
Open up the paper slightly and tuck the corner inside. Close the paper again.

28
Valley fold the top layer from point to point to make the first wing.

USE A RULER!

TUCK IN

29
Mountain fold the left side behind the right side, lining it up exactly with the first wing. Leave the fin sticking out.

FIN

30
Open up the wings and nose flaps on either side. Make sure they are level and the fin is straight.

OPEN UP

FINISHED!

31
Hold the plane in the middle, pull back your arm and give a sharp, straight throw.

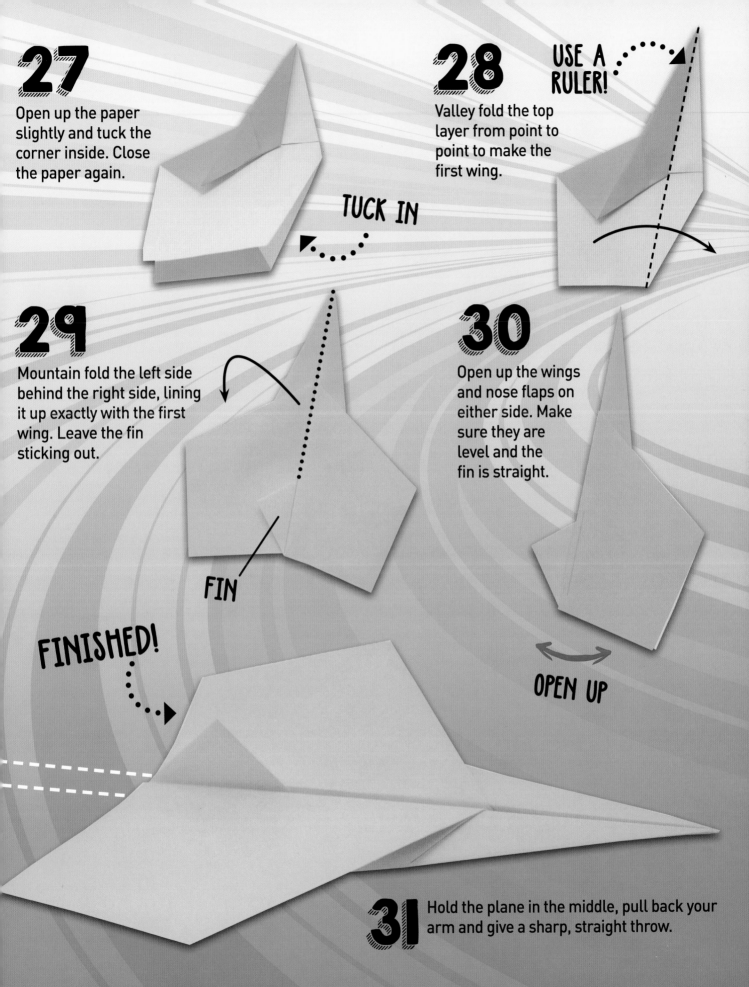

STUNTS
Stunt Planes

Pick your wildest paper to fold these stunning stunt planes and put on a dazzling display of loops, twirls, spirals, and dives!

WILDCAT

JITTERBUG

FOLDING TIP
BUBBLES AND LUMPS MIGHT APPEAR IN THE PAPER AFTER YOU HAVE MADE A FEW FOLDS. SMOOTH THEM DOWN BY RUNNING YOUR FINGER OR A PEN LID OVER THE TOP.

CYCLONE

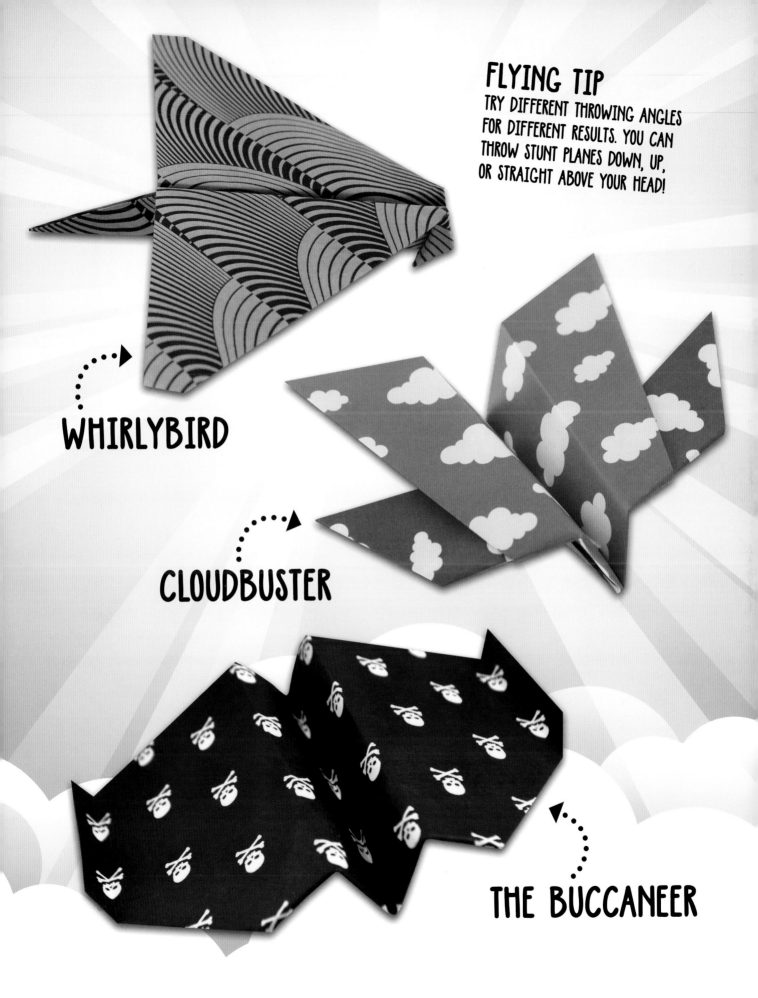

FLYING TIP
TRY DIFFERENT THROWING ANGLES FOR DIFFERENT RESULTS. YOU CAN THROW STUNT PLANES DOWN, UP, OR STRAIGHT ABOVE YOUR HEAD!

WHIRLYBIRD

CLOUDBUSTER

THE BUCCANEER

Wildcat

Fast to fold and fun to fly, this untameable tiger twists and turns in mid-air. If you're planning to ambush your friends, this is your plane!

TURN AND TUMBLE!

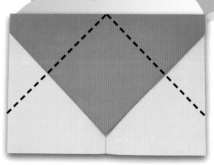

1 Place the paper as shown. Fold it in half from left to right and unfold.

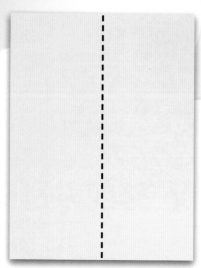

2 Valley fold the top edges to meet on the central crease.

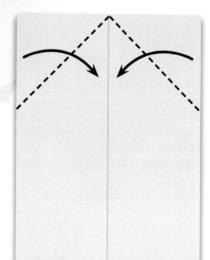

3 Fold down the top point to meet the paper 25 mm (1 in) from the bottom edge.

4 Valley fold the top corners to meet on the central crease.

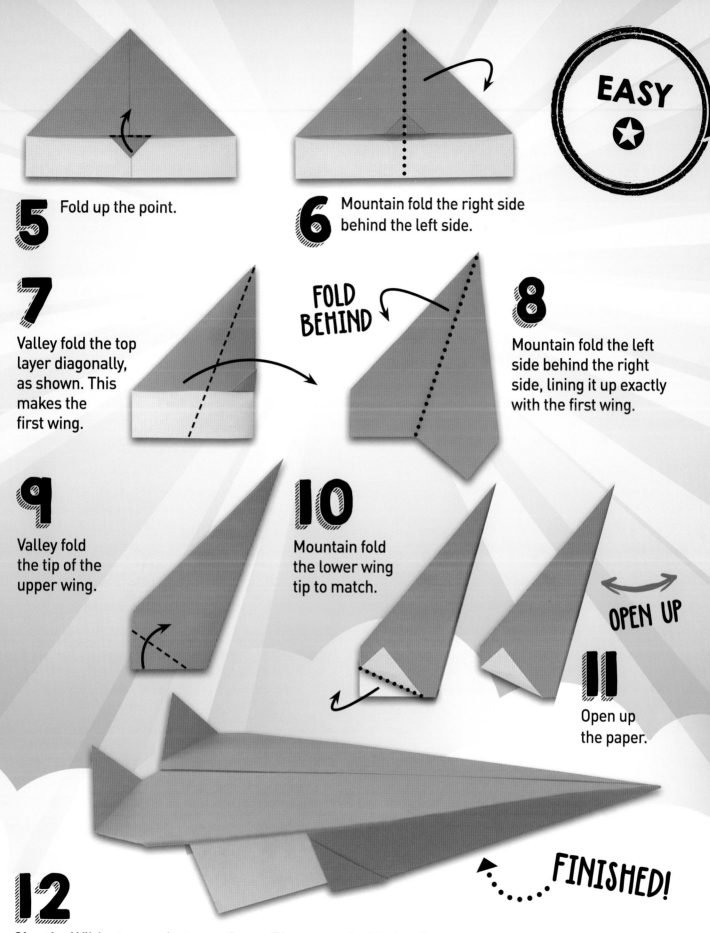

5 Fold up the point.

6 Mountain fold the right side behind the left side.

7 Valley fold the top layer diagonally, as shown. This makes the first wing.

FOLD BEHIND

8 Mountain fold the left side behind the right side, lining it up exactly with the first wing.

9 Valley fold the tip of the upper wing.

10 Mountain fold the lower wing tip to match.

OPEN UP

11 Open up the paper.

FINISHED!

12 Give the Wildcat a good, strong throw. Play around with the tilt of the wings and launch it at different angles to get twists and turns.

Jitterbug

This flighty flyer packs in the stunts. Throw softly and it flits and flutters, or power up for super loops and dizzying dives!

ROCK AND ROLL!

1 Place the paper as shown. Fold it in half from left to right and unfold.

2 Valley fold the top edges to meet on the central crease.

3 Valley fold the top point to meet the bottom edge.

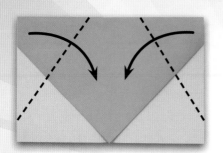

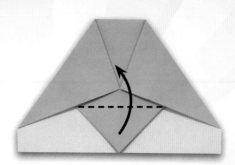

4 Fold in the top points to meet in the middle of the central crease.

5 Your paper should look like this. Fold up the point.

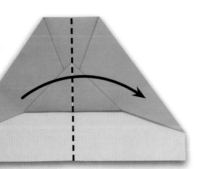

6 Valley fold the paper in half from left to right.

7 Fold back the top layer, as shown. This makes the first wing.

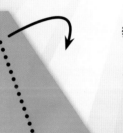

8 Mountain fold the left side behind. Line it up exactly with the first wing.

9 Valley fold the tip of the upper wing.

10 Mountain fold the lower wing tip to match. Open up the wings.

FINISHED! ••••••▶

11 Angle the wings slightly and straighten their tips ready for launch. Vary your power for a range of amazing stunts!

Cyclone

Kick up a storm with this incredible spinning ring. Just give your wrist a twist as you fling to send the Cyclone reeling off into the distance!

FLING AND SPIN!

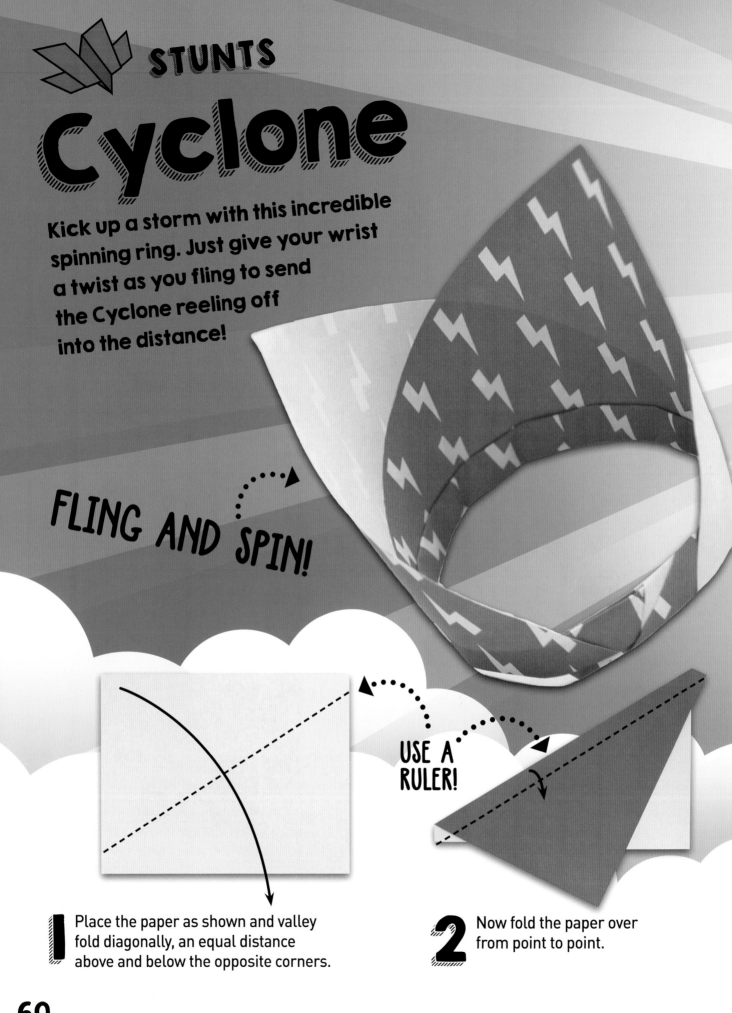

USE A RULER!

1 Place the paper as shown and valley fold diagonally, an equal distance above and below the opposite corners.

2 Now fold the paper over from point to point.

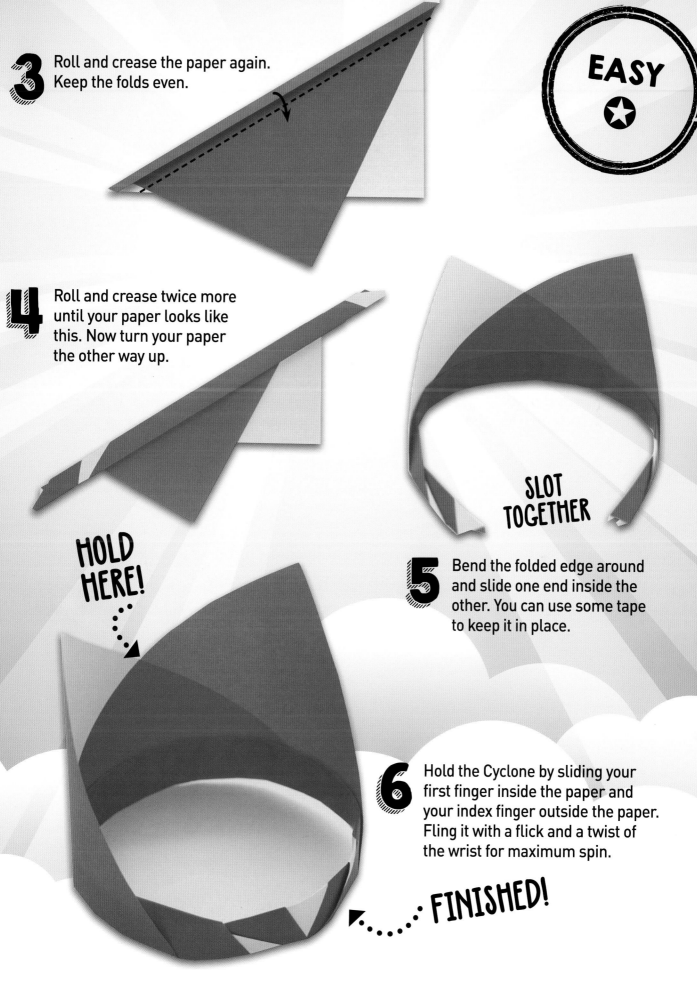

3 Roll and crease the paper again. Keep the folds even.

4 Roll and crease twice more until your paper looks like this. Now turn your paper the other way up.

HOLD HERE!

SLOT TOGETHER

5 Bend the folded edge around and slide one end inside the other. You can use some tape to keep it in place.

6 Hold the Cyclone by sliding your first finger inside the paper and your index finger outside the paper. Fling it with a flick and a twist of the wrist for maximum spin.

FINISHED!

Whirlybird

Q: What looks like a hawk and flies like a helicopter? A: the Whirlybird! Fold its nose right and it will spiral and spin!

WHIRL AND TWIRL!

1
Place the paper as shown. Fold it in half from left to right and unfold.

2
Valley fold the top edges to meet on the central crease.

3
Now valley fold the patterned edges to meet on the central crease.

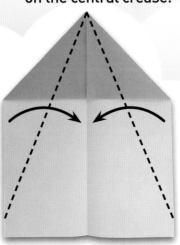

4
Valley fold the point, as shown.

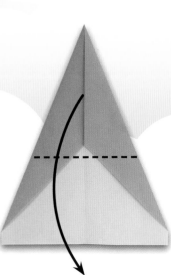

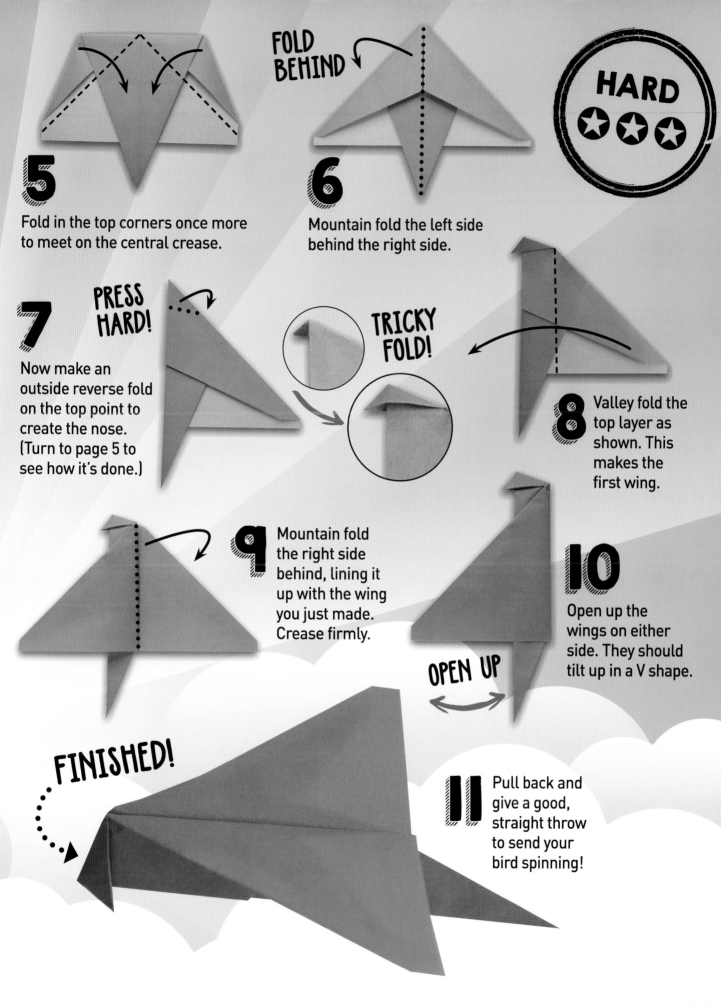

5 Fold in the top corners once more to meet on the central crease.

FOLD BEHIND

6 Mountain fold the left side behind the right side.

PRESS HARD!

7 Now make an outside reverse fold on the top point to create the nose. (Turn to page 5 to see how it's done.)

TRICKY FOLD!

8 Valley fold the top layer as shown. This makes the first wing.

9 Mountain fold the right side behind, lining it up with the wing you just made. Crease firmly.

10 Open up the wings on either side. They should tilt up in a V shape.

OPEN UP

FINISHED!

11 Pull back and give a good, straight throw to send your bird spinning!

STUNTS
Cloudbuster

This cool plane is a breeze to fly. Launch it straight and it lifts, dips, and dives, but angle the wings and it will hang nifty turns!

SWERVE AND CURVE!

1 Place the paper as shown. Valley fold the top edge to meet the right-hand edge.

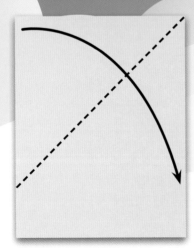

OPEN UP

2 Open up the paper.

3 Now valley fold the top edge to meet the left-hand edge.

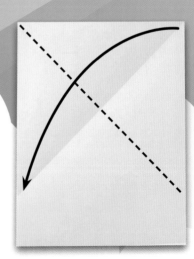

OPEN UP

FLIP OVER

4 Open up the paper.

5 You should now have a creased cross. Turn the paper over.

6 Valley fold the paper over the middle of the cross.

7 Open up the paper.

8 Turn the paper over.

FLIP OVER

9 Push in the sides on the central crease until they collapse.

PUSH IN HERE

PUSH IN HERE

PUSH DOWN HERE

10 Push down on the top of the paper to flatten it into a triangle shape.

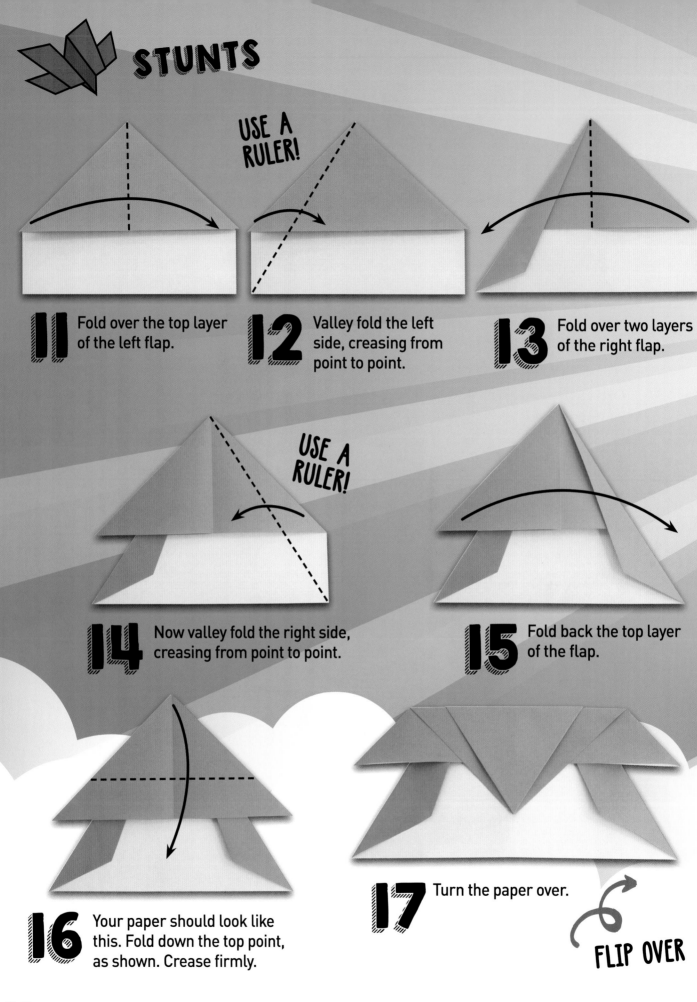

USE A RULER!

11 Fold over the top layer of the left flap.

12 Valley fold the left side, creasing from point to point.

13 Fold over two layers of the right flap.

USE A RULER!

14 Now valley fold the right side, creasing from point to point.

15 Fold back the top layer of the flap.

16 Your paper should look like this. Fold down the top point, as shown. Crease firmly.

17 Turn the paper over.

FLIP OVER

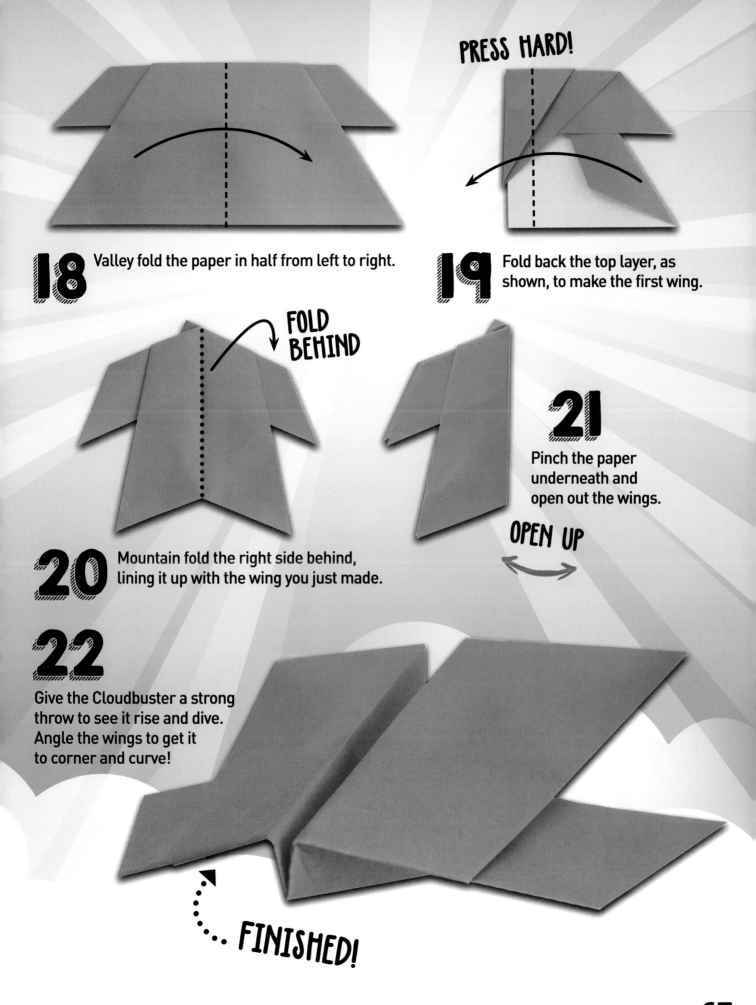

PRESS HARD!

18 Valley fold the paper in half from left to right.

19 Fold back the top layer, as shown, to make the first wing.

FOLD BEHIND

20 Mountain fold the right side behind, lining it up with the wing you just made.

21 Pinch the paper underneath and open out the wings.

OPEN UP

22 Give the Cloudbuster a strong throw to see it rise and dive. Angle the wings to get it to corner and curve!

FINISHED!

STUNTS
The Buccaneer

Win every stunt duel with this swashbuckling flyer. Just send it sailing high into the air for big swoops and daredevil loops!

LOOP-THE-LOOP!

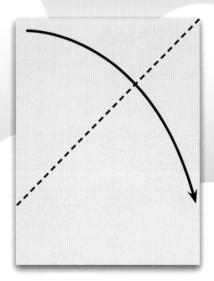

OPEN UP

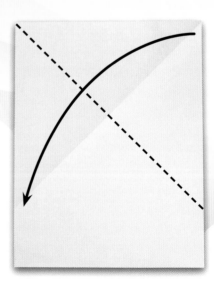

1 Place the paper as shown. Valley fold the top edge to meet the right-hand edge.

2 Open up the paper.

3 Now valley fold the top edge to meet the left-hand edge.

OPEN UP

4 Open up the paper.

5 You should now have a creased cross. Turn the paper over.

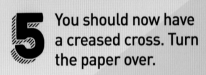

FLIP OVER

6 Valley fold the paper over the middle of the cross.

7 Open up the paper once more.

8 Turn the paper over.

FLIP OVER

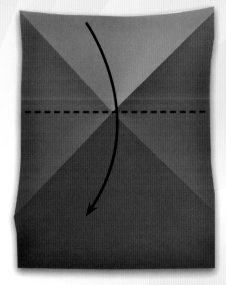

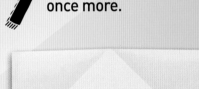

PUSH IN HERE

▼

9 Push in on the central point to make the sides pop up.

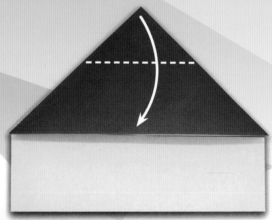

PUSH IN HERE ▶

◀ PUSH IN HERE

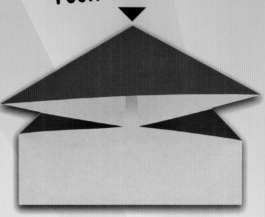

PUSH DOWN HERE ▼

 10 Push in the sides on the central crease until they collapse.

11 Push down on the top of the paper to flatten it into a triangle shape.

12 Valley fold the top point to meet the bottom edge of the triangle.

FLIP OVER

13 Turn the paper over.

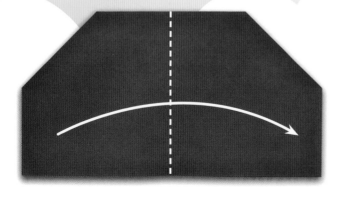

 14 Valley fold the paper in half from left to right.

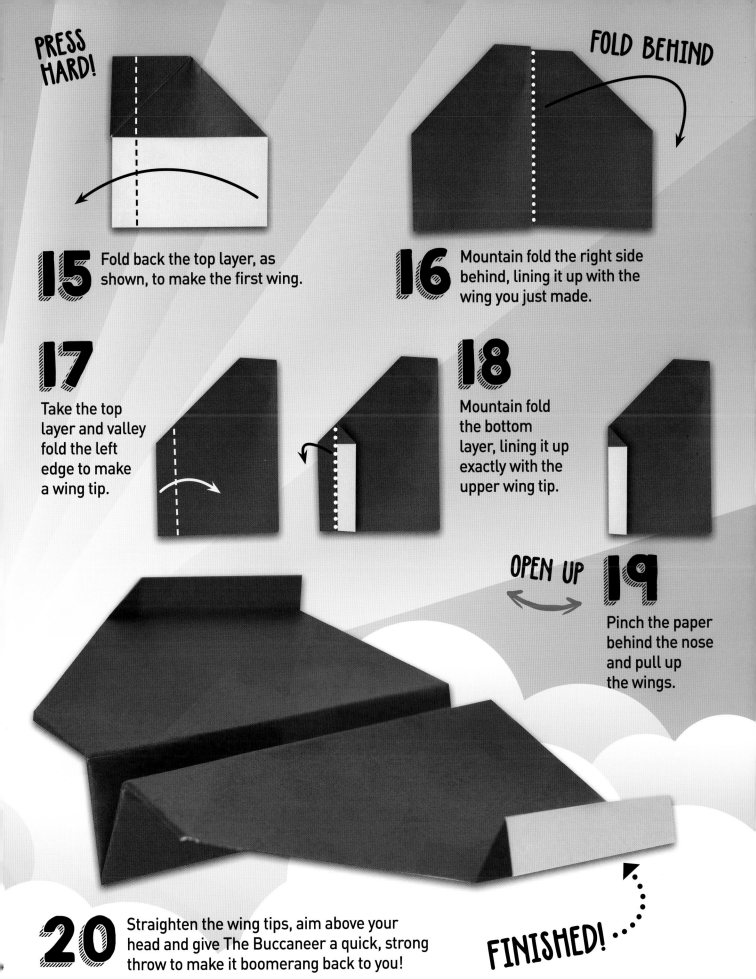

FOLD BEHIND

15 Fold back the top layer, as shown, to make the first wing.

16 Mountain fold the right side behind, lining it up with the wing you just made.

17 Take the top layer and valley fold the left edge to make a wing tip.

18 Mountain fold the bottom layer, lining it up exactly with the upper wing tip.

OPEN UP

19 Pinch the paper behind the nose and pull up the wings.

20 Straighten the wing tips, aim above your head and give The Buccaneer a quick, strong throw to make it boomerang back to you!

FINISHED!

Space Planes

Fast forward into the future with this stellar fleet of space planes. It takes some cosmic creasing and a few smart folds, but you'll soon be ready for blast off!

NEBULA

ASTRAL ORBITER

GALACTIC ROVER

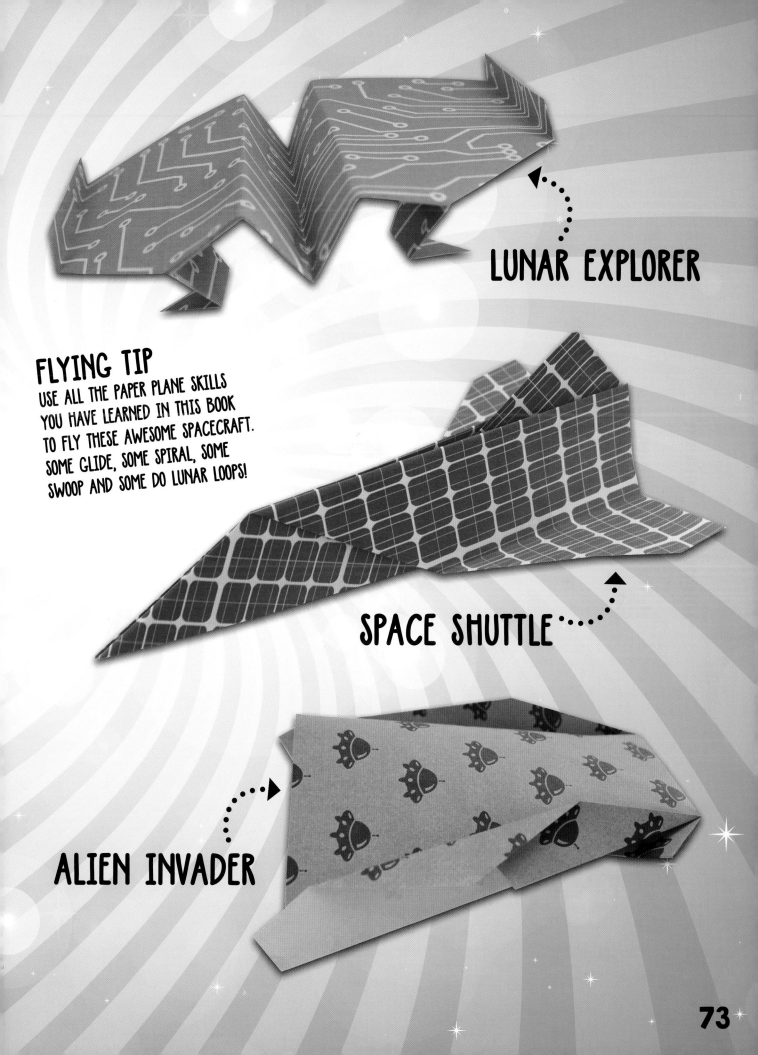

LUNAR EXPLORER

FLYING TIP

USE ALL THE PAPER PLANE SKILLS YOU HAVE LEARNED IN THIS BOOK TO FLY THESE AWESOME SPACECRAFT. SOME GLIDE, SOME SPIRAL, SOME SWOOP AND SOME DO LUNAR LOOPS!

SPACE SHUTTLE

ALIEN INVADER

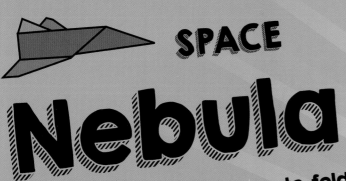

SPACE
Nebula

Get on a roll with this easy-to-fold tube, then test the laws of gravity when you send it spinning through space!

CURL AND WHIRL!

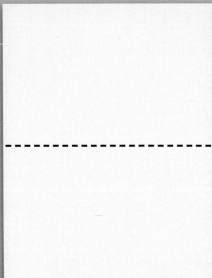

1 Place the paper as shown. Fold it in half from top to bottom and unfold.

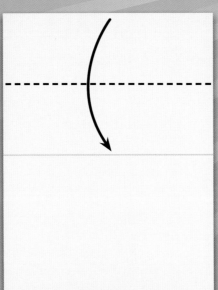

2 Fold the top edge down to meet the central crease.

3 Fold the flap in half from top to bottom.

4 Fold over the top section once more.

5 Hold the paper at either end and pull it back and forth against the edge of a table top. This helps it to curl.

6 Bend the paper round to make a tube.

SLOT TOGETHER

7 Slot one end of the folded edge inside the other.

8 Turn in the folded rim to make it more sturdy. Carefully reshape the tube.

9 Cup your hand around the tube with the folded edge at the front. Aim it upward and throw with a twist of the wrist.

FINISHED!

Astral Orbiter

Aim for the stars with this interstellar spaceship! Fold it right and it will loop in mid-air before floating down for a smooth re-entry.

LUNAR LOOPS!

1 Place the paper as shown. Valley fold it in half from left to right and unfold.

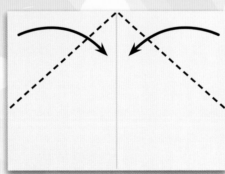

2 Valley fold the top edges to meet on the central crease.

3 Now valley fold the point to meet the bottom edge.

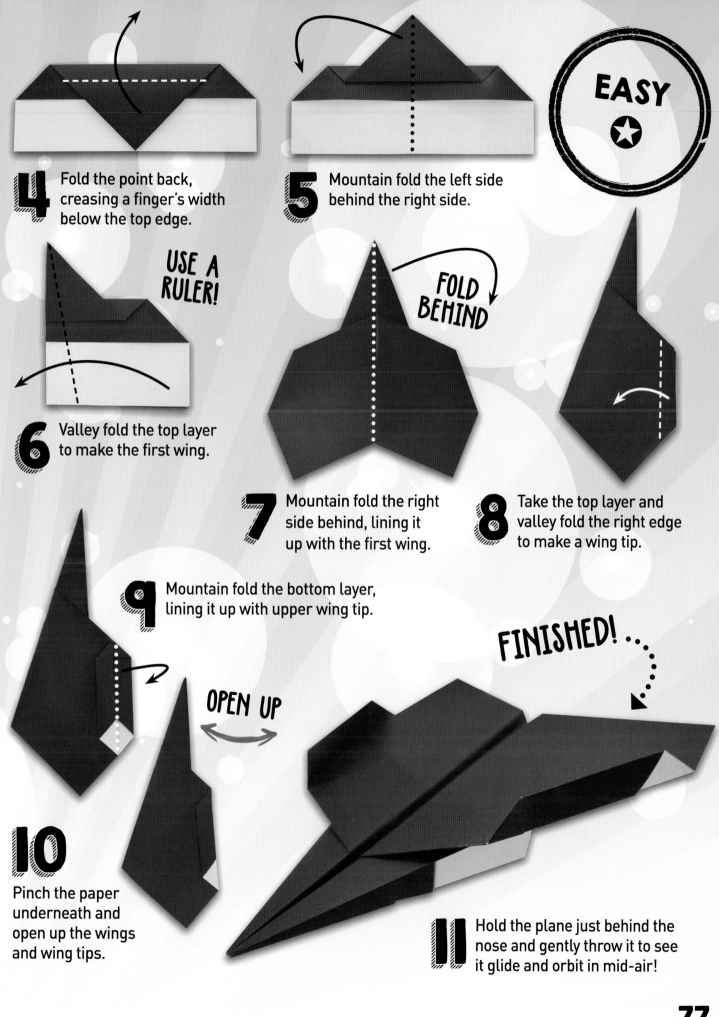

4 Fold the point back, creasing a finger's width below the top edge.

5 Mountain fold the left side behind the right side.

USE A RULER!

6 Valley fold the top layer to make the first wing.

FOLD BEHIND

7 Mountain fold the right side behind, lining it up with the first wing.

8 Take the top layer and valley fold the right edge to make a wing tip.

9 Mountain fold the bottom layer, lining it up with upper wing tip.

FINISHED!

OPEN UP

10 Pinch the paper underneath and open up the wings and wing tips.

11 Hold the plane just behind the nose and gently throw it to see it glide and orbit in mid-air!

SPACE
Galactic Rover

Fold this cosmic spacecraft with its futuristic nose, then send it soaring into hyperspace with a rocket-powered throw!

GLIDE AND RIDE!

1 Place the paper as shown. Fold it in half from left to right and unfold.

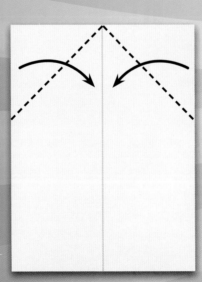

2 Valley fold the top edges to meet on the central crease.

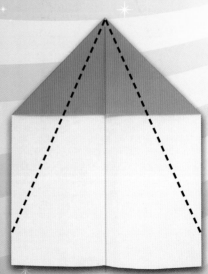

3 Valley fold the sides so that the patterned edges meet on the central crease.

78

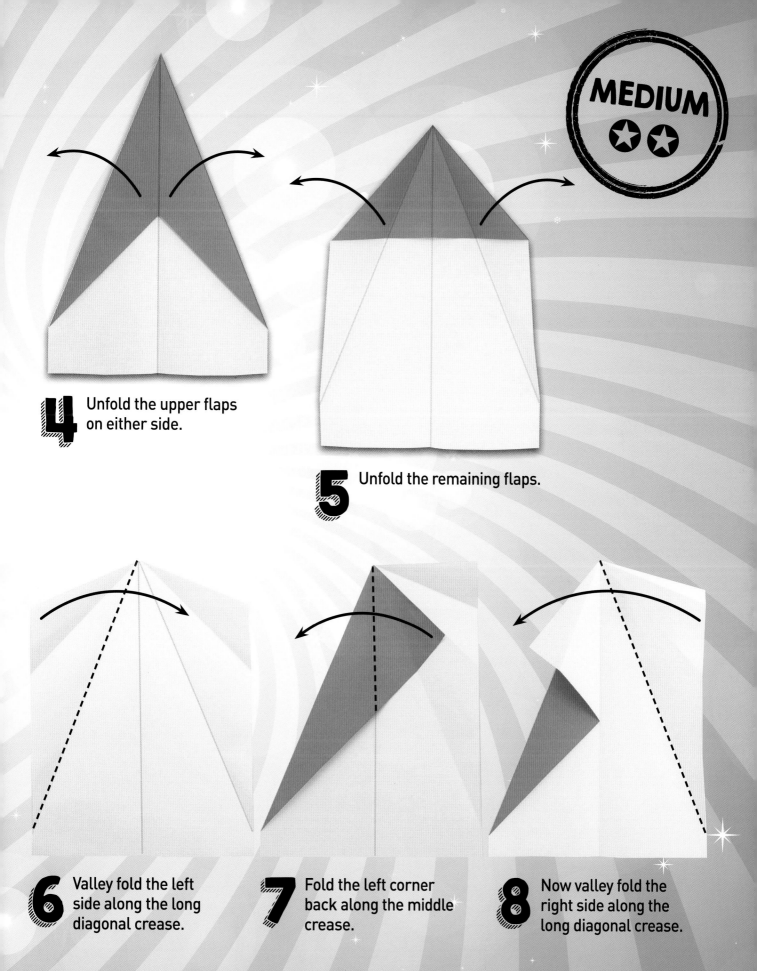

4 Unfold the upper flaps on either side.

5 Unfold the remaining flaps.

6 Valley fold the left side along the long diagonal crease.

7 Fold the left corner back along the middle crease.

8 Now valley fold the right side along the long diagonal crease.

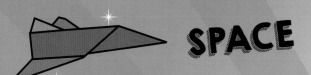

FLIP OVER

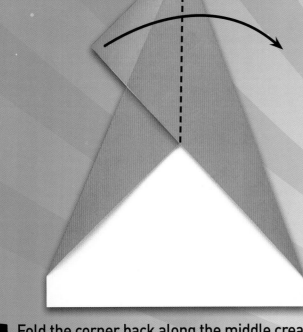

9 Fold the corner back along the middle crease.

10 Turn the paper over.

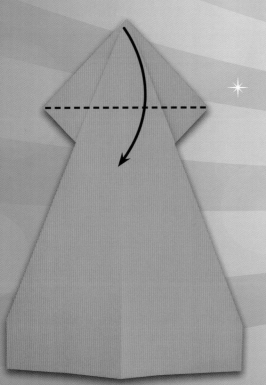

11 Fold the top down, creasing from point to point, as shown.

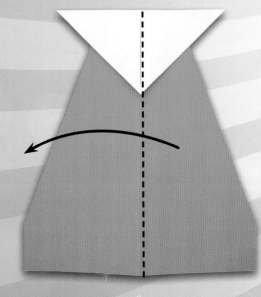

12 Valley fold the paper in half from right to left.

13

Take the top layer and valley fold it to make the first wing.

FOLD BEHIND

14

Mountain fold the left side behind, lining it up with the first wing.

15

Pinch the paper underneath and pull up the wings.

NOSE FLAPS

OPEN UP

16

Open up the nose flaps to make them rounded.

17

Make sure that the wings are smooth and level, then launch your Galactic Rover with a good, straight throw.

FINISHED!

Lunar Explorer

This neat flyer is perfect for space exploration. Fold out its feet for tricky moon landings, or tuck them in to glide through the galaxy!

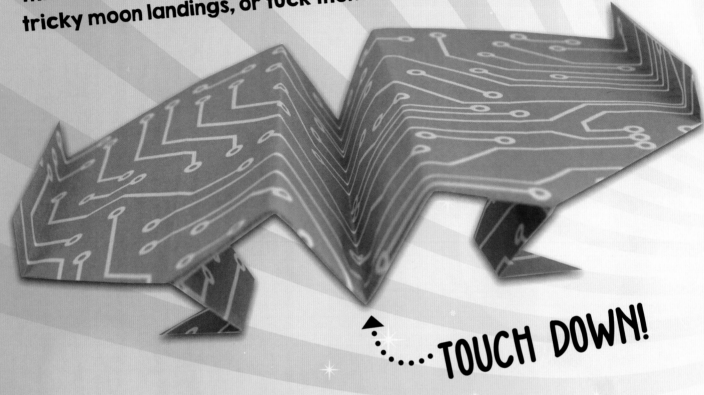

TOUCH DOWN!

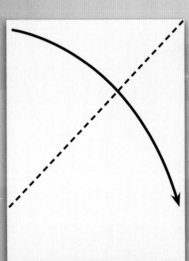

1 Place the paper as shown. Valley fold the top edge to meet the right-hand edge.

2 Open up the paper.

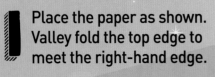

OPEN UP

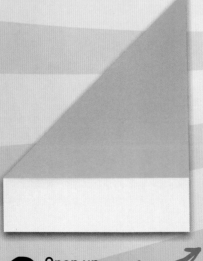

3 Now valley fold the top edge to meet the left-hand edge.

82

OPEN UP

You should now have a creased cross. Turn the paper over.

FLIP OVER

 4 Open up the paper.

5 You should now have a creased cross. Turn the paper over.

 6 Valley fold the paper across the middle of the cross.

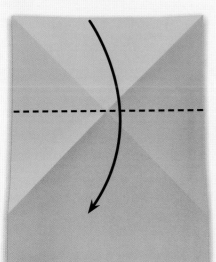

7 Open up the paper again.

 8 Turn the paper over.

FLIP OVER

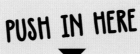

PUSH IN HERE
▼

 9 Push in on the central point to make the sides pop up.

SPACE

10

Push in the sides on the central crease until they collapse.

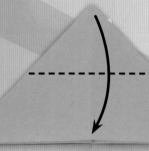

11

Push down on the top of the paper to flatten it into a triangle shape.

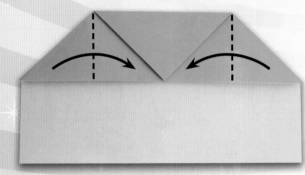

12

Fold down the top point to meet the bottom edge of the triangle. Crease firmly.

13

Take the top layer and fold in the flaps on either side to make an envelope shape.

14

Fold back the flap points to meet the edges of the envelope.

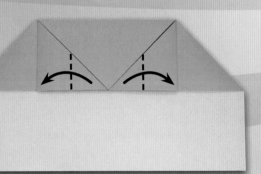

15

Mountain fold the left side behind the right side.

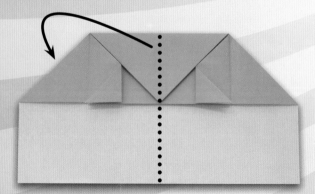

84

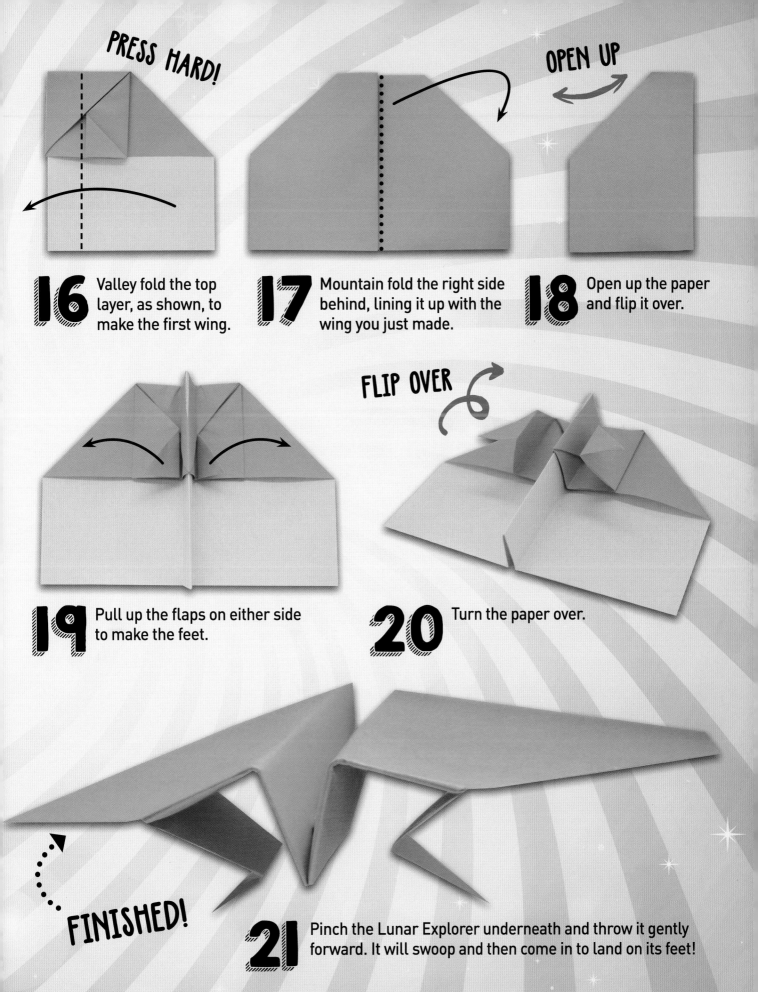

PRESS HARD!

16 Valley fold the top layer, as shown, to make the first wing.

17 Mountain fold the right side behind, lining it up with the wing you just made.

OPEN UP

18 Open up the paper and flip it over.

FLIP OVER

19 Pull up the flaps on either side to make the feet.

20 Turn the paper over.

FINISHED!

21 Pinch the Lunar Explorer underneath and throw it gently forward. It will swoop and then come in to land on its feet!

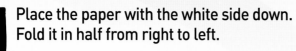

SPACE
Space Shuttle

Make it your mission to fold this cool space cruiser. Begin the countdown to take off, then send it corkscrewing into the cosmos!

BLAST OFF!

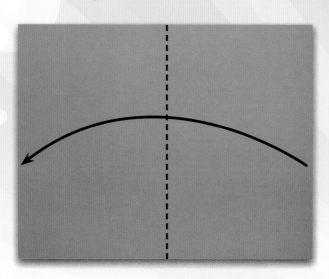

1 Place the paper with the white side down. Fold it in half from right to left.

2 Make an angled valley fold across the bottom right-hand corner.

86

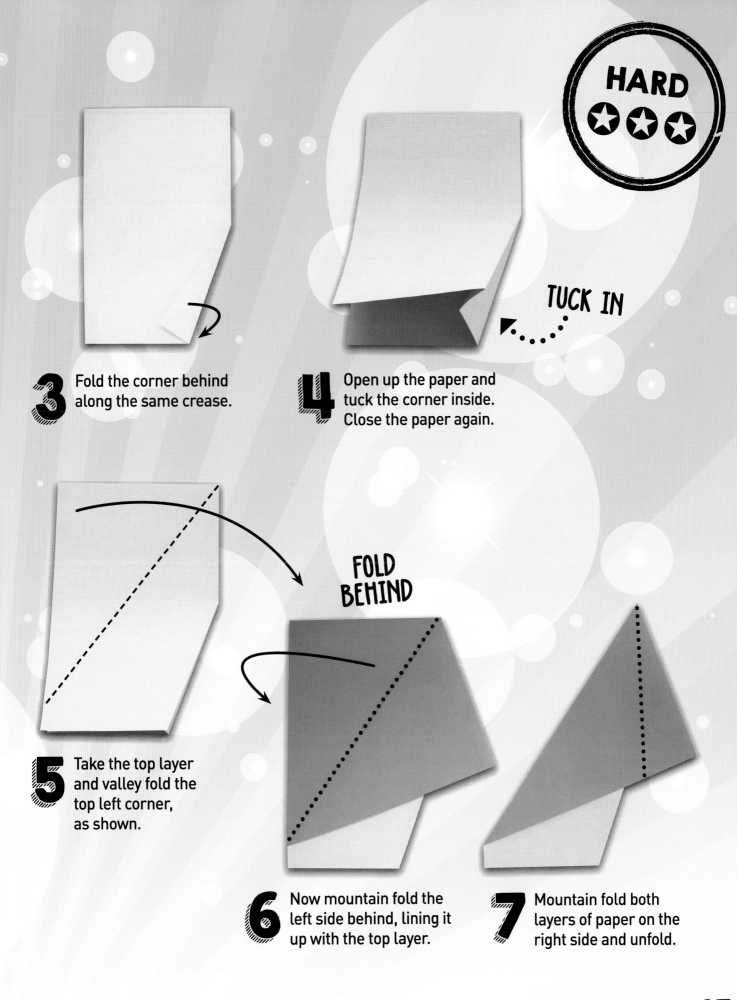

TUCK IN

3 Fold the corner behind along the same crease.

4 Open up the paper and tuck the corner inside. Close the paper again.

FOLD BEHIND

5 Take the top layer and valley fold the top left corner, as shown.

6 Now mountain fold the left side behind, lining it up with the top layer.

7 Mountain fold both layers of paper on the right side and unfold.

SPACE

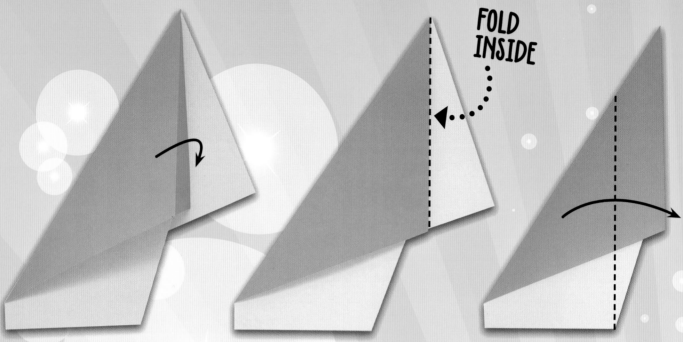

8 Fold the top layer inside along the crease you just made.

FOLD INSIDE

9 Fold the bottom layer inside along the crease.

10 Fold back the top layer, as shown.

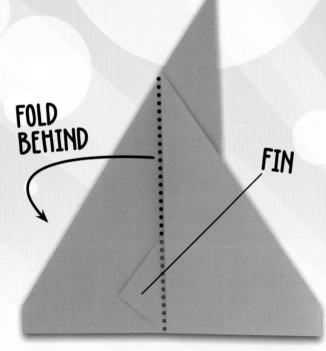

FOLD BEHIND

FIN

11 Mountain fold the left side behind, leaving the fin sticking out. Line up the top and bottom layers exactly.

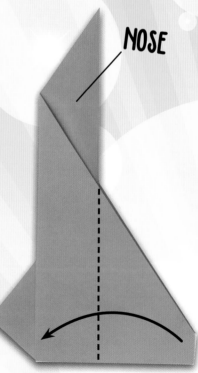

NOSE

12 Valley fold the top layer in line with the nose section. This makes the first wing.

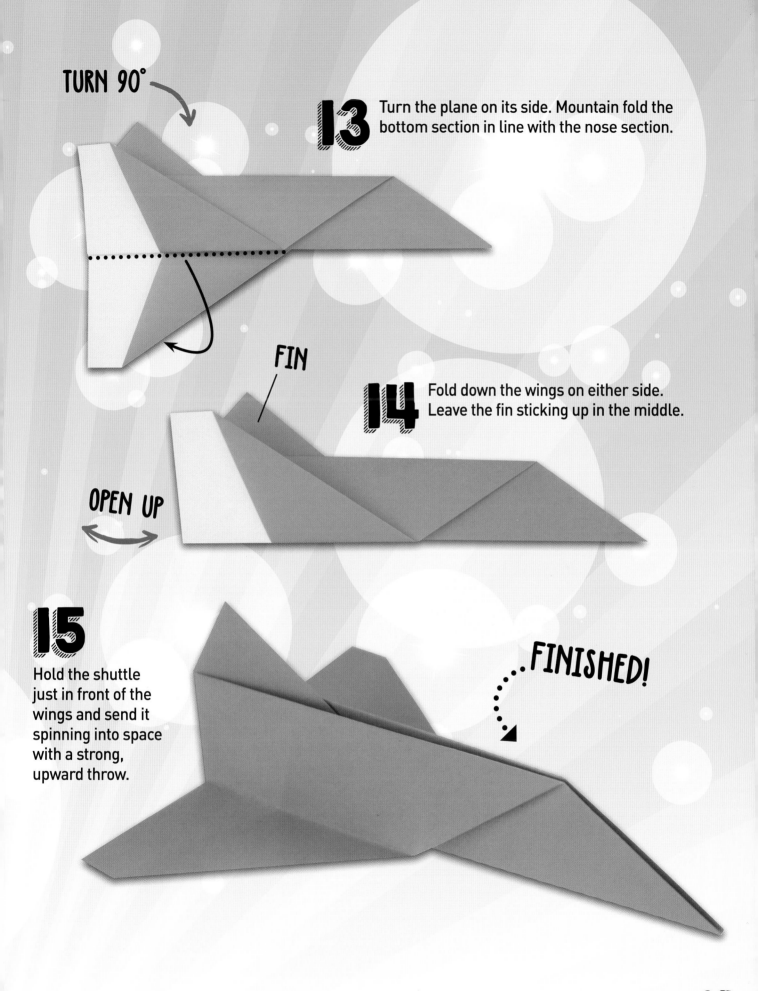

TURN 90°

13 Turn the plane on its side. Mountain fold the bottom section in line with the nose section.

FIN

14 Fold down the wings on either side. Leave the fin sticking up in the middle.

OPEN UP

15 Hold the shuttle just in front of the wings and send it spinning into space with a strong, upward throw.

FINISHED!

Alien Invader

Look out, the Martians are coming! This stealthy UFO swoops silently overhead before diving down for a close encounter!

DRIFT AND DIVE!

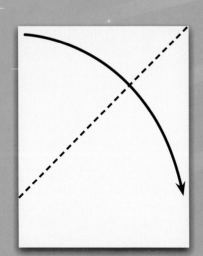

1 Place the paper as shown. Valley fold the top edge to meet the right-hand edge.

OPEN UP

2 Open up the paper.

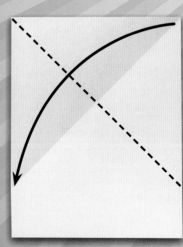

3 Now valley fold the top edge to meet the left-hand edge.

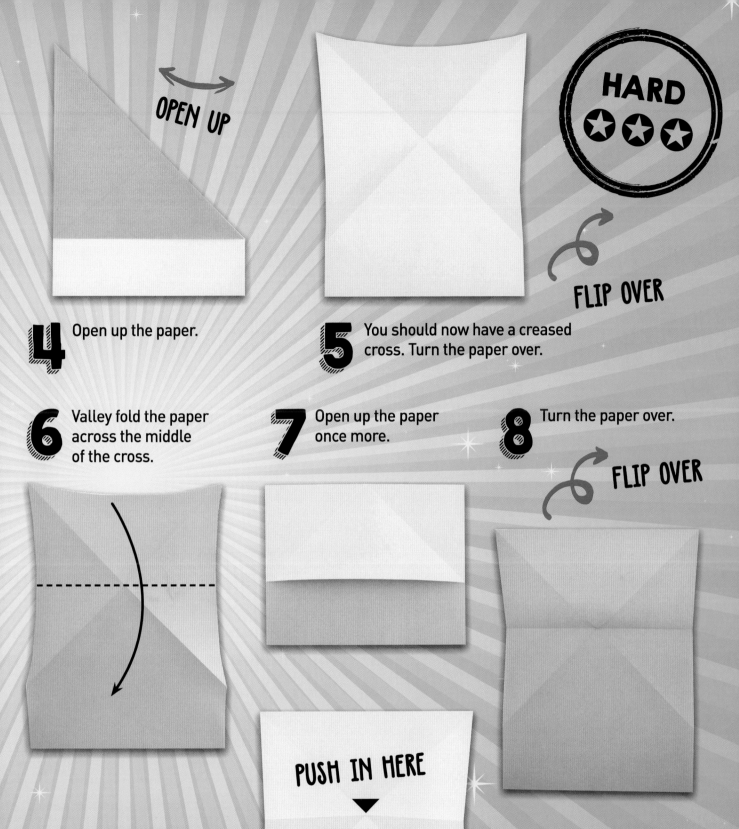

OPEN UP

HARD
★ ★ ★

FLIP OVER

4 Open up the paper.

5 You should now have a creased cross. Turn the paper over.

6 Valley fold the paper across the middle of the cross.

7 Open up the paper once more.

8 Turn the paper over.

FLIP OVER

PUSH IN HERE
▼

9 Push in on the central point to make the sides pop up.

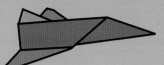

SPACE

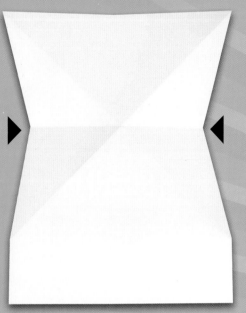

11 Push down on the top of the paper to flatten it into a triangle shape.

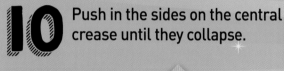

10 Push in the sides on the central crease until they collapse.

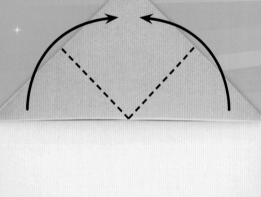

12 Taking the top layer, bring up the bottom points of the triangle to meet the top point.

13 Fold down the top point, as shown.

LIFT UP

14 Lift up the flap that you just made.

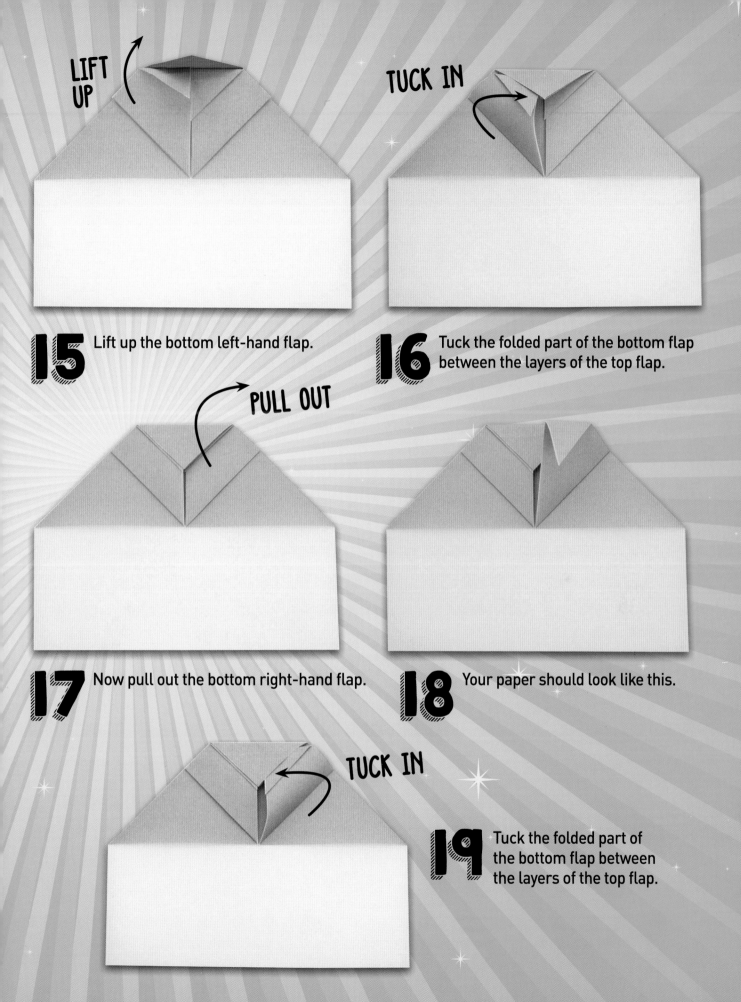

LIFT UP

TUCK IN

15 Lift up the bottom left-hand flap.

16 Tuck the folded part of the bottom flap between the layers of the top flap.

PULL OUT

17 Now pull out the bottom right-hand flap.

18 Your paper should look like this.

TUCK IN

19 Tuck the folded part of the bottom flap between the layers of the top flap.

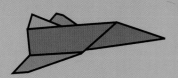

SPACE

FLIP OVER

20 Turn the paper over.

21 Valley fold the left side from point to point. Leave the corner sticking out at the top.

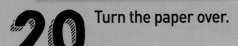

CORNER STICKS OUT

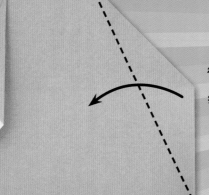

22 Now make a matching valley fold on the other side.

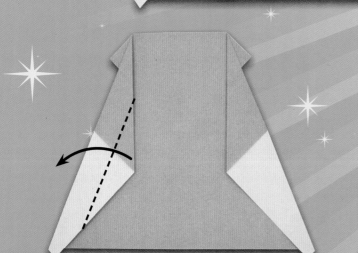

23 Valley fold the left-hand flap, as shown.

24 Make a matching valley fold on the right-hand flap.

25 Put your hand inside the pocket underneath. Open up the pocket to give the model a rounded shape.

POCKET

26 Your spacecraft should look like this. Pull out the wings on either side.

FINISHED!

27 Hold the spacecraft by sliding your hand inside the pocket underneath. Pull back your arm and shoot it forward to send your Alien Invader flying!

Flying Fun

Put your throwing arm through its paces with these fantastic plane games. All you need is a pile of paper and some fellow flyers!

TARGET PRACTICE

Draw a target on a piece of paper and place it on the floor then take 10 paces back. Fold a crisp new plane and see if you can make it land on target. Keep going until you can hit it almost every time!

DISTANCE CHALLENGE

Find the glider that flies the farthest and challenge a friend to a long-distance flight contest. Take five throws each to decide the winner.

THROWATHON

Use the Nebula or Cyclone for this game. It can be played with a group standing in a circle, or with just one friend. Throw your circular plane back and forth between you. Mix up straight throws with spinners and see how many catches you can make in a row.

STUNT OLYMPICS

Pick your ultimate stunt plane and see how many tricks you can pull off in one minute. Try different throwing styles, launch angles and wing tilts to get as many loops, twirls, and corkscrews as you can!